GUARDING ANTONIA (SPECIAL FORCES: OPERATION ALPHA)

GUARDIAN SEALS BOOK 6

NICOLE FLOCKTON

Dear Readers,

Welcome to the Special Forces: Operation Alpha Fan-Fiction world!

If you are new to this amazing world, in a nutshell the author wrote a story using one or more of my characters in it. Sometimes that character has a major role in the story, and other times they are only mentioned briefly. This is perfectly legal and allowable because they are going through Aces Press to publish the story.

This book is entirely the work of the author who wrote it. While I might have assisted with brainstorming and other ideas about which of my characters to use, I didn't have any part in the process or writing or editing the story.

I'm proud and excited that so many authors loved my characters enough that they wanted to write them into their own story. Thank you for supporting them, and me!

READ ON!

Xoxo

Susan Stoker

ACKNOWLEDGEMENTS

A huge thank you to Susan Stoker and Amy Hrutkay for everything they do with Aces Press. Happy to be part of the family.

To the awesome readers who keep picking up the next book in this series. I know you've been waiting for this one and I hope you enjoy Robot and Antonia's story.

Thank you to my great friend Abigail Owen for always listening to me when I'm having a down day and lifting me up when I need it. This writing gig is so much easier with you walking alongside me.

Jennifer, my PA and cover artist, who has created yet another beautiful cover and is always answering my calls when I need help.

Thanks to Courtney at Authors on A Dime for her great copy editing eye and for enhancing this story even more.

As always being able to follow my dreams without the

continued support from my handsome husband Jason, and my two kids who put up with my vague answers when I'm in the zone.

ABOUT THE BOOK

What happens in Vegas stays in Vegas, right? That's what Antonia Rocca thought about her impetuous marriage to a Navy SEAL. When circumstances bring them back in the same orbit, the attraction is still there, even though she does everything to fight it. When it comes to light that their marriage isn't annulled like she'd believed, she's adamant that ending their union is for the best.

Brendan "Robot" Dean is never one to make a rash decision, so his Vegas marriage is very out of character. However, when he discovers it is still valid, he considers it an opportunity to explore his attraction to Antonia and find out if they really could have a marriage. If only Antonia agreed with him.

After Antonia witnesses a murder, Robot is there to provide support and keep her safe and she finds herself seeing him in a way that has her thinking of a future she never imagined. Before they get the chance to find out, Antonia is taken by the murderer. Robot and his team must race against time to save her from becoming his next victim.

For Nicole, a new friend

CHAPTER 1

"We had a one-night stand, Robot. That's all it was." Antonia glared at the man she'd been attempting to avoid for the last twelve months. An impossible task considering her best friend was married to his teammate, meaning they all socialized together. Not to mention she'd moved down to Virginia where they all lived. She should've stayed in New York.

What the hell had she been thinking to move close to her best friend?

She hadn't been thinking. It was as simple as that.

The man in question moved, his shirt pulled tight across his biceps, stretching the fabric until it looked like it would split apart.

Geez, the guy was too damn sexy and it was getting harder and harder to resist him.

But she had to.

God, she wished she could go back to that night two

years ago in Vegas and pick a different roulette table to play at, one where Brendan 'Robot' Dean wasn't.

Why the hell were they having this conversation at T-Rex and Brielle's nuptial celebration?

"It was a bit more than that." He drawled in that low sexy growl of his. "We got married."

"Don't remind me. It was a stupid drunken mistake. A bad sitcom storyline. Besides, we immediately rectified our problem the next day by agreeing to draw up annulment papers. Papers I signed and returned to you the minute they arrived on my doorstep." Antonia blew out a frustrated breath. The last place she wanted to be was in a room where Robot's masculinity cloaked her in a sensual fog she wanted to get lost into.

All it would take would be one step.

One step and then she could lay her head on his chest. Have his arms wrap around her and keep away all the demons she'd been fighting since her teenage years. But she couldn't do that. She needed to be strong and keep her distance from the dangerous Navy SEAL. "I don't see why you have to bring our drunken mistake of a marriage up now?"

"Because we need to talk about us." Robot took a step toward her and she took one back. He couldn't touch her. If he did, she'd cave into the longing she'd been fighting since the moment she walked into his backyard party and clapped eyes on him again two-years after they first met in Vegas. She slammed down the shutters on her thoughts, she didn't need to be thinking about what happened that night in his bedroom.

One stupid mistake after another.

No not a stupid mistake.

Antonia determinedly ignored the little voice in her head. "There is no us. We," she pointed between the two of them. "ended the second we woke up in that Vegas hotel room and the reality of what we'd done sank in."

"If only it was that simple," he muttered and ran a hand over his closely cropped hair. The one thing she'd always admired about Robot was the way he was in control of everything. Looking at him right now, he appeared anything but the kick-ass Navy SEAL team lead she knew him to be.

The ball of dread that formed in her stomach the second he asked to speak to her in private multiplied until it was larger than the boulder Indiana Jones ran away from. Her breaths came out faster and a bead of sweat trickled down her back.

"What exactly are you saying here, Brendan?" She never used his given name. He'd introduced himself to her as Robot and that was how she always thought of him. Antonia was sure he'd told her how he got his nickname, but it was probably while her mind had been full of vodka and lust, so nothing had soaked in that night.

Apart from the mind-blowing sex.

Yeah, she could no longer deny the validity of the voice in her head. Sleeping with Robot was the one thing she wanted to forget about her time in Vegas, and it was the one thing she couldn't. After that weekend she'd made a promise to herself—no more one night stands. What had she done when she'd seen Robot again? Gone and slept with him. Only it wasn't one night, she'd spent the whole weekend in his bed.

The attraction had been hard to deny. Not to mention the way he'd stayed by her side while she'd been in the hospital after her and Erin's kidnapping.

"An assistant from my former lawyer's office called me yesterday the annulment papers were never filed. We're still married." Robot stated as he shoved his hands in his pants pocket.

Blood rushed through her ears, and her heart thudded against her chest. She'd heard him wrong. Hadn't she?

It couldn't be true.

She'd misheard him. She had to have.

They couldn't still be married.

They couldn't.

"Please tell me this isn't true." During their whole conversation she hadn't wanted to believe the niggling thought in her mind that something had gone wrong with their annulment. Call it a sixth sense, but why else would he have brought up what happened in Vegas? What happens in Vegas is supposed to stay in Vegas, not follow her to Virginia.

Warm hands closed around her shoulders and the fight to keep her distance from Robot seeped out of her like a retreating mist.

"I'm sorry, but it is. Seems someone at the office didn't do their job properly."

There wasn't a hint of softness in his tone and that made her even more annoyed. She wrenched away from his hold. "Damn you, Brendan."

She turned on her heel and stormed out of the room not wanting to be close to the man a minute longer. He'd messed her up so much it wasn't funny. For two years she'd managed to push aside her marriage mistake. Hadn't breathed a word of it to anyone. Not even Erin. She and her BFF shared just about everything.

When she'd signed the papers, she'd been positive everything had been sorted out. What she should've done was file them herself, then she would've had the assurance that their one-night marriage was over.

God, Antonia still couldn't believe how stupid they'd been. It wasn't like they'd been kids when they'd stumbled into the chapel attached to the hotel. They were adults with careers. People who should've know better.

"Antonia, don't run away from me." He didn't speak loudly. Like her he didn't want to draw attention to them, but he'd said the words with quiet authority that rankled her already stressed demeanor.

She whirled on him, anger firing through every nerve ending.

"You don't get to demand anything of me, Brendan Dean. I need time alone and," she marched toward him and stabbed him in the chest. "You need to respect that."

His hand closed over hers, trapping it against his warm chest. Beneath her fingers his heart beat thudded a rapid tattoo.

Her breath shortened and the inconvenient desire that always consumed her when she was close to Robot wended its way through her like a meandering river.

"Antonia," he whispered, and the pull of her name on his lips had her lifting her gaze. The look of unbridled heat in his eyes should've had her running as far away from him as possible, except it lured her closer.

In slow motion, his head lowered towards her. Even

knowing what was going to happen, she could do nothing about it because she wanted it as much as he did.

The second his lips touched hers, her upside-down world righted itself. She'd been expecting a ravishing, but she got the opposite. Robot's mouth moved sweetly over hers. A sigh rippled through her and her muscles relaxed as she fell into the kiss. Her trapped hand clutched at his shirt while her free arm anchored itself behind his neck.

This kiss was unlike anything they'd shared before. Their mouths danced together while their tongues remained hidden away from each other. Normally their kisses were carnal, like they were both punishing each other.

The sound of laughter wafted down the hallway, breaking into their spell, reminding them of where they were—in Brielle's father's house celebrating Tim and Brielle's elopement. As well as the births of two babies on Robot's SEAL team. The babies were a few months old now, but the team had been away a lot so they hadn't been able to rejoice in all the recent happenings.

Her breath sawed in and out as she took two steps away from Robot. Everything in her screamed to drag him back to the room they'd been in and scratch the itch that had been a constant companion for the last twelve months since the weekend at his house.

"We can't brush aside what's happening between us anymore, Antonia," Robot said quietly.

She sighed and wrapped her arms around her waist. "I know but give me a couple of days to think this over."

He nodded and shoved his hands in his jeans pocket. Antonia's eyes were drawn to his groin and the outline of the erection she'd felt against her belly during their kiss. "I'll see what else I can find out."

This time she nodded. "I guess we'd better get back before we're missed."

"You go. I need a couple of minutes," he responded and smiled ruefully.

Heat rushed up her cheeks and she turned quickly so he wouldn't see it. She hoped by the time she returned to the living room it would be faded enough so no one would think anything of it.

God, the last thing she needed was for Erin to comment about her pink cheeks. Nothing got past her friend and she'd successfully avoided her questions about Robot over the last year, but soon it would be impossible to achieve that.

Antonia hated keeping secrets from her best friend, but getting so drunk she married a guy she'd only known a few hours was too embarrassing to admit. Not to mention, monumentally dumb. Robot could've been a serial killer, for all she knew. The outcome could've been far worse than an unwanted marriage, though that was still not ideal.

The attraction to Robot had been instantaneous and immediately consumed her, even through the copious amounts of alcohol she'd consumed, yet she still couldn't fathom how she went from the roulette table to the chapel.

Taking a deep breath, she walked back into the living room where the rest of the team were partying. Immediately, her gaze sought out Erin. At the moment, her friend was fully occupied with her new son and hadn't noticed she'd returned to the room.

Another quick look around showed everyone was caught up in their own conversations, except for Brielle. Her attention was fixed totally on Antonia. The other woman chewed her bottom lip and it looked like she wanted to come talk to her.

Antonia's stomach dropped as her sixth sense kicked in again and understanding sank into all of her pores.

Brielle knew.

Shit.

BRENDAN 'ROBOT' DEAN WILLED HIS BODY TO SETTLE down. He wasn't a randy teenager anymore who sported a hard-on at the drop of a hat but being around Antonia had his body ignoring years of rigorous training.

He was a fucking Navy SEAL, he had more control than this.

"Why are you hiding in here?" A familiar voice came from behind him.

"Nothing, I just needed to make a call." Lying to a fellow teammate was very rare for him, but at present the last thing he wanted to do was tell the truth to his teammate and closest friend, Carlos 'Italy' Porcelli.

"Really? Is that why Antonia walked out all flushed and with her shirt half out of her pants?"

Brendan pushed a hand through his hair and blew out a frustrated breath. He and Antonia had been playing this cat and mouse game for months, ever since he'd seen her walk into his backyard when Italy and Erin had first started seeing each other over a year ago.

When he'd heard the name Antonia being bandied around by Italy he hadn't thought it would be *his* T, the woman he'd spent an incredible weekend with in Vegas.

What the fuck? Since when did she become his?

Since the second you laid your lips on hers in that smoke-filled casino and put a ring on her finger.

The voices in his head had their own little discussion. He let them have it because listening to them would only highlight how true his thoughts were.

"Leave it alone, Italy, I'm not in the mood." He went to move out of the room, but a hand shot out preventing his escape.

Brendan glanced down at his arm before flicking his gaze up to the man whose hand rested there. "I suggest you take your hand off me."

"Jesus, Robot, settle the fuck down," Italy groused back at him, but he removed his hand.

Remorse bit at his heels. He shouldn't take his frustrations out on his friend. The reason their team worked like a well oiled machine was because of the way they trusted each other implicitly.

"Sorry, I just need..."

Fuck, he had no idea what he needed. His dick twitched against his zipper letting him know what *he* wanted. Yeah, well he might want it too, but it wasn't happening—no matter how much he wished it.

"Dude, you need to get laid," Italy clapped him on the back. Brendan didn't want to think how closely his friend mirrored his own thoughts. The last woman he'd slept with was the woman he'd just kissed in this room.

One weekend months ago was all they'd had together. The weekend where she'd turned up and he laid claim to her the second he worked out that Erin's Antonia was the woman he'd been married to for all of twelve hours.

Or so he thought.

Finding out that they were still married should've had him running to his former lawyer's office, abusing the shit out of them for their incompetence. Instead, he found he wanted to thank them for giving him a second chance at a marriage that shouldn't have been.

Problem was, it looked like he was the only one who wanted a second chance.

CHAPTER 2

Antonia sipped her cup of coffee and gazed out the window of her second story apartment overlooking the complex's pool. It was certainly a better view than the alley full of dumpsters she'd had in New York.

Sleep had been elusive the previous evening. After escaping from T-Rex and Brielle's party she'd gotten home and wrapped herself up in her favorite blanket, knitted by her Nonna, and stared at the blank television screen while eating a gallon of chocolate ice cream. She didn't trust herself to put the TV on. In her state, her night would've likely included a Hallmark channel binge while she cried into her Ben and Jerry's as couple after couple got their happily ever after.

Like her life needed anymore of those. How was it possible that in little over a year so many of the people she'd met had found their soulmates? While she'd come face to face with her biggest mistake.

Her sexiest mistake.

The best thing that had ever happened to her, if she let it.

Antonia squashed that thought. The less she let herself think about Robot, especially a naked Robot, the better for her sanity.

How could they still be married? It didn't seem possible that a law firm could be so careless as to not file important papers like an annulment with the Court. They were messing with people's lives.

Geez, it was lucky in the two years since that fateful night in Vegas she hadn't fallen in love and gotten married.

God, how embarrassing would it be to be getting ready to marry the love of her life only to find out she was still married. Try explaining that one away. As it was, she'd kept her dirty little secret to herself.

A sigh rippled through her and she finished off the contents of her mug. Shaking off the melancholy that crept into her like an insidious virus since Robot broke the news to her yesterday, this annulment needed to be a priority. After she got ready for work, her first plan of action would be to look up the law firm and see if she couldn't get this mess sorted out herself.

The sound of her cell ringing beside her interrupted the early morning quiet and a quick glance at the screen told her it was Erin calling.

If she picked it up, she'd get the Spanish Inquisition for bugging out of the party early. If she didn't pick up, her friend would probably get worried and send Carlos or someone else over to check to see if she was all right. And with her her luck, it would be Robot turning up on her doorstep.

Antonia snatched the phone up and accepted the call. "Hey, Erin, you're up early."

Seriously? You're just asking for her to play twenty questions with you.

She shushed the voice in her head, so she could focus on what Erin was saying.

"I have a two month old, I won't be able to sleep in for the next eighteen years. Plus, it wasn't too long ago that I was getting up at the ass crack of dawn to go to work."

"True, how is my godson?"

"Cranky. I think he was handed around too much yesterday and now I'm paying for it."

Antonia laughed, recalling the way the big bad Navy SEALS had been passing around both Kieran and Emma like they were footballs. As much as she wanted to deny it, seeing Robot holding a baby, a huge smile on his face had warmed her insides. He would make a great father.

Just not a father to her own child.

Liar.

"Maybe you should get Carlos to look after his son today and you can go get a massage or something," Antonia said in an attempt to douse the image of Robot and a blue eyed baby.

"Oh, I would love that," Erin sighed. "But it's not possible, he's already left for the day."

Hearing the tiredness in her friend's voice, Antonia came to a decision. "How about I call the office and say I'll be working from home today and come over and watch Kieran?"

A loud sniff sounded down the line. "You'd do that for me?"

"Of course, I would. You're my best friend. I got your back."

"You've been hanging around SEALS too long, Toni," Erin responded, tears clogging her voice.

It took a second for Antonia to comprehend what Erin was saying. "Takes one to know one."

Yeah, that was a path she didn't want to travel down and examine too closely. She looked out the window again, leaning closer to the glass. A flash of the early morning sun glinted off something metallic looking.

What is that?

She squinted as if that would help her to focus on what she thought she saw. There, in the far corner of the pool deck by the changing rooms, hidden by the short squatty trees, she could make out a couple. They appeared to be having an argument. The woman's face was obscured so all she could make out was one denim clad leg and part of her pale pink top. Antonia had no idea if she was a resident or not.

The guy was muscular, also wearing jeans, with a black t-shirt that had some sort of emblem on the back, but she was too far away to make it out. He had longish dark hair which fell across his face.

She'd lived in New York long enough to know the best thing to do when confronted with something like this—look away and ignore whatever the hell was happening. This situation looked threatening and one she would be wise to let play out without getting involved.

"Run," Antonia whispered, though in her head she was yelling. It appeared like the woman's assailant had her in a tight grip. The guy looked around and up in Antonia's direction quickly before facing the woman again. Her grip tightened around her mug and her stomach churned a little.

Had he seen her?

Did he register anything when he looked her way?

Like watching a replay in slow motion, Antonia saw the guy raise his arm, a wicked looking knife in his hand confirming the flash of steel she thought she saw earlier had been real and not a figment of her imagination.

A gasp escaped out of her as he plunged the knife into the woman, before pulling it out and repeating the action over and over. The coffee she'd just drunk swirled and tumbled in her stomach. Bile rose up in her throat and she swallowed hard, pushing it back down.

"Oh my God. Oh my God," she cried out. The words echoed in her mind even after she'd finished saying them.

As if the guy who'd just killed a woman in cold blood heard her cries, he looked up again in her direction as he wiped the knife on his shirt. A self-satisfied smug smile on his face.

For half a heartbeat, she was frozen to the spot as if cold ice had crept out of the floor and wound around her feet. She finally came to her senses and ducked down behind the kitchen counter, hoping and praying he hadn't seen her. Bile rose in her throat as her heart pounded so violently she worried it would pop out of her chest. Her rasping breaths were harsh and erratic.

"Antonia! What's wrong." The cries came from far away. She looked around and saw her phone had slipped from her grasp and lay on the tiled floor beside her. Her fingers trembled as she reached over to pick it up.

"I-I-I think I just saw someone murdered," she whispered, as if afraid the guy was going to hear her and come for her.

"What?" Erin's high-pitched screech had her pulling the phone away from her ear. "Are you serious?"

"Yes." Antonia pulled her knees up, resting her head on them not sure what to do. As much as she wanted to look out the window again, she didn't want to risk being seen, in case the guy was still hanging around. But she couldn't let her fear stop her from confirming what she thought she'd seen.

"You need to be a hundred percent sure you saw what you did, Toni. This is serious." Her friend sounded in control of herself now. The calm tones exactly what she needed.

"Tell me something I don't already know."

"Did you see who did it? Can you identify the person if you have to?" Erin peppered her with questions. Questions she didn't want to answer, but knew she had to.

"I only caught a quick look at him. I don't think he saw me, but I can't be certain. My mind is blank at the moment."

She closed her eyes and thought for sure that would help her to picture the guy's face, but there was nothing, just black as if her mind had totally wiped the event from her memory bank. She blinked a few times and her kitchen came back into focus.

Had another resident seen it as well? Or was she the only one? Maybe it wasn't what she thought it was. Maybe he didn't really stab the woman, and it was one of those fake magician knives that retracted when coming in contact with the body.

Yeah, that works because you totally didn't see him wiping blood on his shirt.

Well, at least she knew her sarcastic inner voice was on the case. Maybe she could get her subconscious to deal with it.

A hysterical laugh bubbled up inside of her and she swallowed it down. Laying her head against the kitchen cupboard, she wished she'd stayed in bed. Tossing and turning would've been preferable to the situation she now found herself thrown in.

"Toni, are you still there?" Erin's insistent voice blew through her desire for her morning to start off differently.

"Yeah, I'm still here."

"Where are you exactly?"

"In my kitchen. I thought I might look out the window again."

"I'm not sure that's a good idea. I think I should let Carlos know what's going on."

"No," Antonia exclaimed. God, the last thing she wanted or needed was her apartment overrun by Navy SEALs, because she knew Carlos wouldn't turn up alone. After yesterday, she didn't need to see Robot, not when her mind was in flux over the news he'd dropped on her.

"Geez, Toni, why are you being so stubborn? You said you saw a murder! And that you think the person who did it saw you. Being alone is the last thing you should be."

Yes, Erin was right, but then again, she had no idea if the guy really saw her or not. "Look, maybe I mis-interpreted what I saw. It may not have been a knife."

Hadn't she already been through this scenario with herself? The excuse sounded pathetic. She could totally picture Erin rolling her eyes at her.

Okay, enough was enough. She'd never cowered from anything in her life and she wasn't about to start now. She stood up and braced herself to look out the window, hoping against hope that she wouldn't see a dead body.

"Fuck." No such luck.

"What?"

Antonia sighed. "I see a body. I'm going to call 9-1-1. I'll talk to you later." Without waiting for a response, she disconnected the call.

She had no idea if someone had already called but it wouldn't matter. Now, she had no choice, and couldn't ignore the reality of the situation—she'd witnessed a murder.

Ten minutes later, she was pacing her small kitchen, her glance continuing to go out the window. The first scream from a resident had come while she'd been on the phone to the 9-1-1 operator. Fortunately, someone had alerted the building super and he'd come out to make sure no one got too close to the victim and not muddy the crime scene.

God, she'd been watching too many crime shows if she knew stuff like that.

Her heart leaped into her throat when a loud pounding echoed around her apartment. Logically, she knew it would be the police but a part of her feared that it was the murderer and he'd found out which apartment she lived in.

Wiping her sweaty palms down her jeans she

approached her front door tentatively, attempting not to make any sound in case it was the killer and not the police.

Looking through the peephole, a mix of relief flowed through her. It wasn't the murderer, but two cops, one in uniform and a woman in plain clothes.

She opened the door with hand still shaking. "Good morning, officers. Thanks for coming so quickly."

"Good morning, I'm Detective Janet Correa and this is Officer Kirk Patterson. Are you Antonia Rocca? And did you call about a suspected murder in the courtyard?"

"Yes, that's me. And yes, I did." She stepped to the side. "Please come in."

The two crossed her threshold and before she shut the door, she looked down the hallway in both directions. Nothing but the narrow grey carpeted hall and closed doors.

Sighing to loosen her tense shoulders, she closed and locked her door, then secured the chain.

They still stood behind her and she pasted a smile on her face as she faced them. Was that stupid to smile in the midst of a murder investigation?

Her nerves were tumbled together tighter than a ball of yarn. "Um, do you want to come through to the kitchen?" She had no idea what to do, and, for the first time in recent memory, she wished she had someone beside her. Someone she could lean on and take point on this interview.

An image of Robot flashed in her mind, but she quickly banished it. She couldn't afford to let herself get too close to him. It didn't matter that they had a piece of paper saying they were married, they were as far from a married couple as Piglet and Eeyore.

"The kitchen is where you witnessed the suspected homicide?" Detective Correa asked. Seeing as she was the one doing most of the talking, Antonia assumed she was taking the lead on the investigation.

"Yes, come this way." She brushed past the officers and strode down the hallway into the kitchen.

Detective Correa walked straight over to the window and gazed out. "So, you were standing here when you witnessed the crime?"

"Yes, ma'am. I was drinking a coffee, talking to my friend on the phone. I glanced out the window and thought I saw a glint of metal. I leaned a little closer and then saw a couple arguing."

"Did you get a good look at them?"

Antonia noted that Officer Patterson had pulled out a notepad and was taking notes.

"Well," she started and then paused, closing her eyes again to see if she could conjure up the events of an hour ago. Vague pictures flashed across her mind. For some reason her mind wasn't letting her remember all the little details. Perhaps she was trying too hard. "I couldn't really see the woman, she was hidden by the trees. And I know the guy looked up, but at the moment my mind doesn't seem to be cooperating with me to remember everything."

The cops nodded, and Officer Patterson made some more notes. Detective Correa peered out the window again, before turning to her. "If you—" she broke off when a loud pounding on her front door echoed through the apartment.

The police's demeanor changed in a flash, both straightening, their hands going to their holstered guns. "Wait here, ma'am," Officer Patterson stated.

Before she could respond there was another loud knock before. "Antonia, it's Robot, let me in."

"Oh geez," she groaned. Of course, it had been wishful thinking to assume Erin wouldn't have told Carlos what had happened. And no way would Carlos not have told his team lead. They'd probably been together when Erin called.

"You know this *Robot* person?" asked Officer Patterson.

"Yeah, he's a friend. Let me go let him in before he breaks down the door." She rushed out of the kitchen down the hallway, pulling the chain and unlocking the door. The second she opened it, six burly men stormed into the apartment. She plastered herself against the wall to stop from getting trodden on.

"Looks like you have your own protection detail, ma'am." Detective Correa commented with a wry smile.

Antonia swallowed the words she wanted to blurt out, instead she smiled and nodded. What she had was six interfering men who always had to be in control.

If the SEAL team had any regrets for the way they barged in, they didn't show it. Her apartment wasn't huge to start off with, but with Robot's team and the two police officers standing around, it felt more like a matchbox.

"Okay, SEAL team, go into my living room while I finish up with the police. I'll deal with you in a few."

The men smiled before heading her request. All but Robot, who widened his stance and crossed his arms over his chest, giving the impression of an immovable rock wall. She narrowed her eyes at him and cocked her head to indicate he follow his team. His lips firmed into an even straighter line.

Damn him, he wasn't budging. Did she really think he would?

Maybe not, but she hoped he might.

"Is he bothering you, ma'am?" Detective Correa asked, and she had to bite back a laugh at the image of the police officer trying to remove a Navy SEAL.

Robot took two steps until he was standing by her and he stared down the cop. "I'm her husband. I'm staying."

Antonia gasped at Robot's admission. "What the hell do you think you're doing?" she hissed at him. She looked around to make sure none of his team heard him. Thankfully the area was empty, but her apartment wasn't huge, and Robot hadn't done anything to keep his voice down.

Great, this day was getting worse and worse.

"If you're her husband, why weren't you here with her this morning?" The detective looked around the room. "There's no indication you reside here. Why should we believe you, considering Ms. Rocca's reaction to your declaration?"

Well, Antonia could be thankful the police hadn't immediately taken Robot's word as gospel.

Robot shrugged his impressive shoulders. "It's a long and complicated story, but the fact of the matter remains, I'm legally her husband and I'm staying with her while you question her further."

"Ms. Rocca can you confirm this, please? Is this man your husband?"

Talk about being pushed into a corner with no way out, but Antonia had no plans to lie to the police officers and end up in trouble. “Yes, he’s my husband. Technically.”

Shit, that felt so weird to say out loud. And oddly...right.

The detective turned her attention back to Robot and the two stared each other down until Detective Correa finally nodded her head. “Fine, we’ve only got a couple more questions anyway.” She directed her attention back to her. “If you saw some mugshots do you think you may be able to recognize the man you saw?”

And just like that, she was transported back to the reason why there was a SEAL team and two cops in her apartment. Her breathing became erratic again. Her stomach churned and a sick and sudden feverish feeling came over her. Even though she didn’t want to admit it, Robot had provided a few minutes reprieve from the nightmare her world had sunk into.

A warm hand slid around her waist as if he could sense her distress. Her breathing returned to normal and her churching stomach settled down. Unconsciously, her body melted into the side of his, drawing on the quiet strength he was gifting her. “I don’t know. Maybe.”

“You said you got a look at him earlier,” the detective responded.

“Yes, and I know I did. I just can’t recall anything of what I’ve seen. My mind appears to have blanked it out.”

Robot’s hand started moving up and down her back and it was as distracting as it was comforting. “It’s not unusual for this happen, Detective,” Robot said, his voice deep and commanding. “It’s happened to me before, but after a few hours everything seems to filter back in. I'm sure, in Antonia's case, things will come back to her."

God, she actually didn't want to remember. She was glad her mind had forgotten all she'd seen. But a woman was dead and for all intents and purposes, she was the only one who could help the police.

What she didn't need, though, was for Robot to come in and take over everything. A botched filing by a lawyer doesn't give him the right to believe he could think and speak for her.

Pulling away from his hold, she straightened her spine and faced the police. "Maybe coming down and looking at photos will jog my memory."

The officers looked between her and Robot, she could imagine the millions of questions they had running through their minds. As Detective Correa commented, there was no indication anywhere she was a married woman, and yet, there was an immovable rock standing beside her claiming to be her husband and a living room full of Navy SEALs.

"Right. Well, we'll need you to come down to the station to make a statement anyway. When you do that, you can look at some photos then." Detective Correa reached into her pocket and held out a business card. "Here are my details. Call me today and set up a time, sooner rather than later."

Before she could take the card from her, Robot took possession of the white rectangle. "I'll make sure she comes down today."

Antonia clenched her fists by her side and grabbed

onto her temper to stop it from exploding out of her. No way was she going to lose it in front of the police.

Once again, the cops looked between them and took a couple of steps back. "I'll look forward to seeing you again. Good morning, ma'am, sir." They nodded at Robot and her and headed to her front door.

Good manners pulled her from her internal struggle and she followed them down to the door, determined to have the last word and to let them know that she beat to her own drum, no one else's. "Thanks for coming so promptly, officers, and I apologize for the intrusion."

Detective Correa half smiled at her. "As I said, looks like you have your own protection detail, which, under the circumstances, could be a good thing."

"Yes, I'm a lucky girl, aren't I?" She responded, sarcasm dripping from every word. Typical attitude, believing that because she was alone, she needed protecting. Well, she knew how to fire gun. Had her license and her own weapon hidden away in a safe in her closet.

They both nodded and walked out the open door. Antonia shut it and leaned back against it, closed her eyes and blew out a deep breath.

Her ordeal was far from over but having the police leave gave her a few seconds reprieve where she could believe that her life wasn't up shit creek.

Knowing she couldn't stand against the door all day, she opened her eyes and locked on the figure looming in the hallway. In a flash her anger and indignation returned.

"What the hell did you think you were doing barging in here and telling the police you're my husband."

The jerk had the arrogance to just lift one shoulder nonchalantly. "It's the truth—you're my wife."

"What the fuck? You guys are married? When did this happen?"

Antonia glanced over Robot's shoulder and saw Cowboy standing behind him. Great, just fucking great, now their secret was out.

Having heard Cowboy's exclamation, one by one the remaining members of Robot's team crowded into the small hallway.

"Is this true?"

"You, sly old dog."

"Suzie, is not going to believe this."

"Erin is going to part pissed and part happy."

Antonia had had enough. "Shut up, the lot of you," she shouted. "I want you all to leave, now."

The last thing she needed, or wanted, today was a discussion about her Vegas mistake with Robot's team.

Unfortunately, they were a stubborn bunch and didn't look like they were planning on going anywhere.

She planted her hands on her hips. "Seriously, I want you to leave now. Get. Out. Of. My. Home."

A whole range of emotions began to seep into her: anger, annoyance, fear. Her body began to shake and she had to lock her knees to prevent herself from collapsing to the ground. Tears began to well up and she bit down on her lip to hold back the sob that was about to erupt out of her. Crying in front of these guys wasn't an option. They'd never leave. She had to squash all these unwanted, but necessary, emotions down and wait until they'd left before letting them fall.

As if they could sense that she was at breaking point, one by one, the men began to file out of her apartment. Each one touching her lightly on the shoulder. She found comfort in their support, but it didn't mean she wanted to explain everything to them.

Only one person remained, and Antonia didn't need a flashing billboard to tell her who. She *sensed* him with every fiber of her being. The connection that had been forged that night in Vegas and reinforced every time they were close to each other, tugged at her.

"I'm not going to leave you alone, T." The words were spoken on a whisper, but they may have well been yelled out loud.

The fight flowed out of her like water over a waterfall. What was the point? Deep down she wanted him here. Had been relieved when he'd shown up on her doorstep.

She nodded and then let the threatening tears, she'd been trying hard to keep at bay, tumble down her cheeks.

CHAPTER 3

NOTHING PAINED Robot more than the sight of a woman crying. When that woman happened to be the one woman he'd fought feelings for the past two years, it was worse than when a bullet had ripped through his arm.

Robot closed the distance between him and Antonia and pulled her into his arms. Having her warm and soft body tucked into his felt so incredible after all this time, although, he'd have preferred this moment under different circumstances.

His heart had dropped to his feet when Italy had told him about Erin's phone call and what Antonia had seen. They'd been in the middle of running through an extraction exercise and Italy shouldn't have answered his phone, but ever since Erin had the baby, he always answered her calls. Joker was the same with Suzie. He'd never been more grateful for their bucking of the rules. Just the thought of Antonia being in danger turned his blood cold.

He hadn't thought; he'd only acted, and his team followed.

How far had the team come in a year—one married, two engaged and two kids born. Well, two married members if you counted him and Antonia.

Her sobs were slowing down and, if he knew Antonia, and he did, she'd be pulling away from him at the first chance. He had no plans on letting that happen. She may fight him, but she wasn't going to go through this alone. Now, whether she'd let him help her was another thing.

"You're safe, T. Nothing is going to happen to you. I won't let it." He kissed the top of her head, the fine strands of her dark hair tickling his nose. He inhaled and welcomed the scents of lemon and peppermint that would forever be known to him as Antonia's fragrance. He never thought the two scents would go together, but the sweet and tart aroma fit Antonia perfectly.

"Let's sit down," he suggested. They were still standing in the hallway. When she gave no indication of hearing what he suggested, he tightened his hold and picked her up, carrying her to the living room.

He settled them on the couch and she snuggled into him. Robot relished the complete trust she was granting him. Another indication she wasn't quite aware of what she was doing. Shock at the morning's events had clearly sunk its claws into her and wasn't releasing her anytime soon.

He continued with the slow strokes up and down her back until the tension seeped out of her. Her body softened against his and her breathing slowly evened out. He glanced down to see she'd fallen asleep.

Robot relaxed into the cushions, adjusting Antonia so she was in a more comfortable position. He had no plans on leaving her today. He would escort her to the police station and sit by her side while she gave her statement and looked through the mugshots.

His phone buzzed, and he maneuvered his hand from around Antonia's back to his pocket. The sender of the message was no doubt one of his team, most probably Italy seeing as he was the closest with the guy. The fact they were married to best friends would cement the friendship even more.

That is if Antonia stayed married to him.

He pushed that thought away and studied his phone.

Spoke to Commander Black about the situation. Didn't mention you being a married man, figured you could do that. But he's okay with you spending the day with Antonia. Call me when you can.

He fired off a quick response.

Thanks. I'll keep you apprised of the situation. She's asleep on me at the moment. I think everything got the better of her. When she wakes we'll head down to the police station. Do me a favor and don't tell Erin about what you heard. Let Antonia do it.

A few seconds later his phone beeped with another response.

I'll see what I can do. I think Joker and T-Rex may have already told Suzie and Brielle, but I'll tell them to ask the girls to keep it quiet.

As much as Robot wished for the guys not have said anything to their partners, he had an idea that neither one of them kept secrets from each other. As hard as it would be for Suzie and Brielle, he believed they would keep his and Antonia's marriage between them until they knew for sure Erin had been told.

THANKS. APPRECIATE IT. LATER.

Antonia stirred in his arms and he tightened his hold. She'd be waking soon and then he'd have to convince her to let him come with her to police station.

When he'd received the email from his former lawyer's office about the mix-up, he'd been royally pissed off. Now he was grateful for their fuck up.

"Robot?"

He looked down and saw Antonia was awake, her brown eyes dreamy from her short nap. "Yeah, T, I'm here."

No sooner had he finished speaking, her body stiffened then she pulled away and hopped off his lap. His fingers itched to bring her close again, but he closed them in a fist. Antonia didn't like to show vulnerability to anyone, most especially him.

"How long was I," she waved her hand toward him, "there."

Robot stood and frowned when she took a step back. What? Did she think he would hurt her? Fuck, didn't she know that would be the last thing he would ever do?

"Not long." He checked his watch. "About fifteen minutes."

She nodded and crossed her arms over her chest, tightening the t-shirt she wore, outlining her breasts. He'd never forgotten how their weight felt in his hands. How they tasted on his tongue. His dick hardened against his pants.

Great, the last thing he needed was to be sporting a hard-on when he was trying to show her support.

"Right. I'd like you to leave now. I need to shower then go to the police station. Can I have the detective's card please?" She held out her hand.

If she thought, for one minute, that he was going to let her go to down to the station by herself, she had another think coming. However, coming right out and disabusing her of that notion would only cause them to fight, which would get them nowhere. He needed to let her think she was getting her way.

Robot reached down and picked up the white rectangle and handed it to her. Her eyes widened in surprise at his quick acquiescence of her request. "Make sure you call and go down today."

Antonia took the card from him. "Thanks. I want this over and done with as quickly as possible."

Neither of them moved, their gazes locked on each other. In the depths of her brown eyes, he was sure he spied longing. Like she wanted him to take over, but she didn't. He wanted to take the look away. He wanted to let her know he would never let anything happen to her.

She headed for the door, her intentions loud and clear—she wanted him to leave. "I appreciate you and the guys coming over, even though it wasn't necessary."

Giving her the impression he was granting her wish, he strode past her to leave, stopping in front of her. He waited until she looked up at him. He smoothed a stray lock of her chestnut hair off her face. "Call me anytime. I don't care if it's fucking three in the morning. You hear something, or need me, I'm here. Do you understand?"

Her eyes narrowed at his command to her, but he needed her to understand she didn't have to do this alone and there was no shame in leaning on him. He just hoped she wasn't too stubborn to listen. Though, stubborn or not, he would be at the police station waiting for her.

Giving her the space might be what she wanted, but he knew recalling the events of what she'd seen was going to be harder than she ever imagined.

He'd witnessed people being debriefed after they'd been held captive, recounting what they'd seen and been through, was traumatic. No way was he going to let Antonia experience the fear alone.

"Fine," she eventually said after their silent battle of the wills. "But don't wait up because I probably won't need you."

To any other man those sharp words would cut them down, but he'd been around her long enough to let them bounce off him, like water flowing off a duck's back.

"Make sure to lock the door after me. I won't leave until I hear it click in place."

She rolled her eyes, but a hint of a smile touched her lips. "Fine." He was beginning to think that was her favorite word.

He leaned in and placed his lips softly over hers. "Bye, T.

Robot stepped out and the door shut, he waited half a heartbeat before hearing the locking mechanism engage and the slide of the chain in its track.

He probably had enough time to head back to his apartment, change and get down to the station before Antonia got there.

Surprising her wasn't going to go down well, but tough, his job was to protect against all foreign and domestic terrorists. What happened today may not have been a terrorist act, but his woman needed protecting and he wasn't going to walk away from that.

TAKING A DEEP BREATH, ANTONIA OPENED HER CAR DOOR and stepped out into the Virginian sunshine. The day was mild and she needed the blue skies to remind her of good things after what she'd witnessed that morning.

During her shower, snippets of what she'd seen returned to the forefront of her mind. She hadn't forgotten; her brain was finally letting her process everything after dealing with the shock. Now, she wasn't sure she was happy with her brain. It had been blissful to close her eyes and see nothing but blackness. Now all she saw was a man's knife-wielding arm rising up and down repeatedly.

Not to mention the fact that her brain relived the moment Robot revealed their marriage to the team. She'd been surprised to see that her phone hadn't blown up with text messages from Erin, let alone Suzie. Brielle already knew. She may not have said anything to Antonia, but yesterday it had been clear from the expression on the other woman's face that she'd overheard Antonia and Robot's discussion. Antonia was grateful for her silence, but now that the cat was out of the bag, why wasn't she texting her either?

At least, if there were incoming messages, she could ignore them, but the silence was deafening. There was no way Erin wouldn't be demanding answers if she knew. Surely, Carlos would've told her what he'd heard.

Okay, she'd worry about spilling her Vegas mistake to her best friend later. First and foremost, she had to give her statement. Once that was done, she hoped she could leave the whole mess behind her. A jab of remorse at her callous thought hit her. A woman had died today. A family was mourning the loss of a daughter, sister, aunt, and maybe even a mother. It fell on her shoulders to help make sure the family got closure by helping the police with their investigation. She shouldn't brush what happened aside like a piece of trash.

Enough procrastinating the sooner she walked into the building the quicker she'd get it over with. Making sure the car was locked she headed toward the front of the police station, her steps slowing when she spied a tall figure leaning against the stair railing. To the average onlooker he appeared to be relaxed, but to Antonia, he was on red alert, observing everything around him. Searching for any signs of danger and ready to spring into action.

Of course, he would be here. If she hadn't still been in the depths of shock, she would've worked out that he'd given up far too easily when she'd asked him to leave.

Annoyed that he believed she couldn't do anything by herself, she marched over to him. When she got within touching distance, she poked him in the chest. "What are you doing here? I thought we had an agreement, I'd call if I needed you. As far as I can recall, I haven't called you because I don't *need* you."

She went to jab his chest again, but his big hand

closed over hers, pinning it to him. "I thought about it and decided that you shouldn't do this alone. So here I am."

She rolled her eyes. Did he really expect her to believe him? He'd made up his mind before he left her apartment that he would be with her when she made her statement. "Do you think I came down in the last rain shower? You had this planned."

He shrugged his shoulders and she gritted her teeth in frustration. God, he was so annoying. And why couldn't the man look ugly? Dressed in black pants and an ice-blue shirt that only highlighted his eyes more, he could be posing for GQ magazine, not waiting to enter a police station with her.

As much as she wanted to fight him for being a presumptions dick, deep down she was glad he was here. Brave as she thought she was, the thought of giving her statement was tying her up in knots. Having him by her side would give her the strength she needed to get through it all.

But there was no way in hell she was ever going to let him know that. It was a little secret between her and her mind.

"Fine." The word erupted out of her. It was becoming her favorite word when responding to anything he said. "Let's go."

She turned and walked to the front door, her heels clicking out an impatient tattoo. Before she could get her hand on the handle, Robot's was there, opening the heavy glass door for her. Damn the man, and his gentlemanly ways. Why did he have to be so appealing? How many women would like to have a big sexy SEAL by their side? A lot.

The thought of seeing him at any of the team's get-togethers with another woman spiked a flash of jealousy so hot inside of her she was surprised steam didn't come out of her.

Their lives were so complicated now. Had become that way the second she stepped into his backyard all those months ago. She'd been going to meet Joker, but the moment she spied Robot, standing tall and looking all powerfully delicious, all thoughts of hooking up with Joker had flown out the window. As it turned out, they were never meant to be anyway because Joker was meant for Suzie, and she was still married to the man walking beside her.

"When this is done, we need to sort out filing the papers to annul this joke of a marriage." She stopped in the middle of the hallway and turned to him, hands on hips. "And speaking of our *marriage,* I can't believe you blurted it out to the rest of the team that we were married. Why would you do that?"

"Now is not the time, nor the place, to discuss it." She opened her mouth to protest but he held up his hand, stopping any response from her. "I'm not saying we don't need to discuss it, because we do. All I could think about was getting to you and making sure you were okay that when the cops asked me why I was there, it just popped out."

Popped out, my ass.

But he was right, the middle of the police station wasn't the place to air their dirty laundry. "I suppose you're right, but we will talk about this. I can't believe it's been complete radio silence from the girls. I've got a bad feeling about that."

"I asked Italy not to say anything to Erin."

"What? Why?" Shocked that he would do that.

"Because I figured it would be better coming from you than him."

Again, with the consideration to her feelings. The man was confusing. Or rather, he was confusing her.

"Well thank you, I appreciate it."

He nodded and they continued on their way to an officer at the front desk who directed them to the row of hard plastic seats lining the wall.

"I really don't want to be here," she muttered as a sudden chill swept over her.

Robot's arm landed around her shoulder, pulling her into him. "It's okay, I've got your six. You're not alone."

A sigh shuddered out of her and she placed her hand on his hard thigh. She needed him more than she ever thought she would.

THE SUN WAS LOW IN THE SKY WHEN THEY WALKED OUT OF the building a few hours later. Her eyes hurt from looking at page after page of mugshots. After a while, all the faces seemed to meld together until they all looked alike.

"Well, that was a waste of an afternoon," she muttered as she they walked down the stairs.

"Not really, you gave them a good statement with some good descriptions."

She scoffed at Robot's words. "Good description? I couldn't give them anything. Now this woman is dead, and her killer is running loose." A shiver wracked her body at the thought and Robot put his arm around her bringing her close to him.

She'd never been more grateful for Robot's presence in her life than she was at this moment. He hadn't said much at all while she'd given her statement or looked at the pictures. He seemed to be able to anticipate her every need. A drink would turn up beside her when she needed it. Or a hand would rub soothing circles on her back whenever she got overwhelmed.

Antonia paused at the bottom of the steps and turned so she could look at him directly, dislodging the arm that held her to him.

"Everything, okay?" he asked quietly, reaching out to take both her hands.

"I couldn't have got through this without you, Robot. Thank you for being here for me."

"T, there was never any other place I'd be today other than by your side. It was no hardship."

Antonia believed every word. "God, I wish I had stayed in bed this morning then I wouldn't be in this situation."

Robot pulled her tight against him and, as his arms enclosed her in his warm embrace, she rested her head against his chest and clung to him. The last thing she wanted was to go back to her empty apartment, but she was also too afraid to ask if she could go to Robot's place, which was utterly ridiculous because it wasn't like the guy would say no.

Maybe she could go to Erin's.

No. She squashed that thought quickly. Erin had a new baby and didn't need a stressed out friend hanging around. Not to mention she could potentially lead a murderer to her best friend's house.

"Oh shit," she said as she remembered what she'd promised her best friend this morning.

Robot went rigid beneath her fingers. His muscles tightening, ready to spring into action. "What? What's wrong?"

"I was supposed to look after my godson today so Erin could get a massage. I was talking to her and making arrangements when it all happened. She sounded so tired and I wanted to help. Some friend I am."

He chuckled, and the sound rumbled through her warming her insides. "I'm pretty sure she's okay with you letting her down. Besides, I think Italy was taking half the day off so he could look after the baby and she could go pamper herself."

Antonia wasn't sure if that was true or not, considering Erin hadn't mentioned it that morning, but maybe Carlos had been planning to surprise his fiancée. "Still, I probably should call her, I haven't spoken to her since this morning. And," she sighed heavily. "I guess I need to tell her about us."

How much had her life changed in the last twenty-four hours. Was it just yesterday they'd been standing in a room in Brielle's dad's house? It seemed so much longer.

"Do you want me to come with you?" he asked pulling away a little so she had to look up at him. The intense sincerity in his blue eyes was almost too much to take, yet utterly perfect at the same time.

Would having him by her side be easier to break the news to her friend or would it be a hindrance?

What she did know was, she didn't want to be alone and he was offering to be with her for a little longer.

"Yeah, I think I would."

He leaned forward and kissed her on the tip of her nose. "I'll call Italy and give him a heads up. Where are you parked?"

"In the lot across the street. What about you?"

He'd pulled his phone out and was holding it up to his ear. "I got an Uber here. Hey, Italy."

Antonia stared at him, sure her mouth was hanging open. He *Ubered* to the police station? Had his plan all along been to go home with her? So what if it was? It was what she wanted. She may not have known it when she arrived at the station, but she sure as shit knew it now.

She tuned out Robot's conversation. He'd told her he'd asked the guys not to mention anything and with the brotherhood between them on the team, she believed Carlos hadn't said anything to Erin about her marriage.

Antonia jumped when Robot's hand landed on the small of her back. "You ready to go, T?"

She opened her purse to dig her keys out. "Yeah, let's go."

"Can I have the keys please?" His question was asked in the softest of tones, as if he was afraid she was going to shatter into a million pieces.

"Why?"

"I'm driving." His tone brooked no argument. She may be tired, but she could most definitely drive her own car.

"I don't think so. I've seen the way you drive. I'd like to get to Erin's place in one piece."

"Be reasonable, Antonia. You've had a traumatic day. You're tired. Let me drive. I promise I'll drive carefully."

She snorted at that. "Right, you don't even know how to drive carefully. You guys are all the same, zipping in and out of traffic, stopping so close to the car in front it's amazing you're not kissing bumpers."

He laughed. "And you drive so slow it's amazing there aren't cobwebs on your car by the time you get to your destination."

"Oh, ha ha ha. Just because I don't go ten miles over the speed limit like you do, doesn't mean I drive slow. I'll have you know that I drive five miles over the limit."

He closed the small gap between them, his fingers closing over hers which were clutching her keys. She looked up and her breath caught. His eyes were ablaze with humor, something she'd never seen him in before. It was a heady look she could definitely get drunk on.

The outside noise seemed to disappear and all her focus zeroed in on the man standing in front of her. The humor in his eyes faded and was replaced by desire, their color going a darker blue. She was trapped, and she didn't want to escape. The attraction between them was as hot and as intense as it had been that night in Vegas, and then again, a year ago, at his house.

His free hand came up and framed her face. Her nipples peaked against her bra and heat suffused her body.

"Antonia," he breathed before he closed the gap between

them. She helped him by going up on her tiptoe and their lips melded together. His mouth was gentle on hers, so different from the first ravishing kisses they'd shared the night they'd met. Then, all they wanted was to consume each other.

She wound her arms around his neck and pressed her body closer to his. He was hard to her soft.

Before she was ready for it to end, Robot pulled away from her and rested his forehead against hers. "We should go. When I talked to Italy he said he wants us to come over. Erin's worried about you. She's left you a ton of messages, apparently."

Antonia pulled herself out of the trance she'd fallen into with Robot's kiss and took a couple of steps away from him. Her fingers touched her swollen lips. She'd always lost her track of time when they kissed. The last two kisses they'd shared seemed different—more meaningful than any of the other ones they'd shared.

She pushed aside the fanciful thoughts. Her emotions were all over place, which meant it was the worst time to even think about what feelings she was experiencing by being with Robot again.

Taking a calming breath, she reached into her purse and extracted her phone from the side pocket. The second the screen lit up, it was full of notifications. She smiled ruefully and held it up for Robot to see. "I put my phone on silent when I got into the car to come to the police station. Guess I should've thought about checking it earlier."

He stooped to pick up her keys. She hadn't known she'd dropped them, but the second Robot's lips had landed on hers, her mind had focused only on him. "You can read and answer while I drive us."

The thought of arguing with him flashed across her mind before she immediately dismissed it. If she was being truthful, she didn't want to deal with rush hour traffic. "Fine, you win this time. But I'll be driving myself home."

He gave a non-committal grunt and she rolled her eyes. Now this was the Robot she was very familiar with.

CHAPTER 4

"Are you ready for this?" Robot asked as he turned the engine off and they sat in Erin and Italy's driveway.

Antonia had been quiet the whole drive from the police station to their house. Not surprising considering the afternoon she'd had, plus she'd been busy dealing with her text messages.

At least she had a little more color in her face now. When they'd walked out of the police station, she'd been pale and her normally fiery brown eyes were dull and murky like the mud flats they'd spent hours in during BUD/s training.

"As ready as I'll ever be." She unhooked her seatbelt and faced him. "It's not like we have any choice. We can't quietly dissolve our marriage now seeing as you blurted it out to your entire team."

The last thing he wanted to do was get into an argument with Antonia in Italy's driveway. She may think she was feeling better after everything she'd been through, but she'd forgotten he'd held her while she cried out her shock. He'd been by her side while she recounted everything she'd seen for the police. Hearing her describe the way the man had repeatedly stabbed that woman made his blood run cold.

The missions he'd been on over his career as a SEAL hadn't been pleasant and he'd seen many atrocities against women. He'd divined great pleasure in shooting the balls off many guys who'd raped innocent women and children. He'd gladly shoot this murdering bastard in the balls, if he ever found him, just for scaring his woman.

"Robot, are *you* okay?"

Antonia's voice pulled him from the dark thoughts he'd fallen into. He didn't often think about all he'd seen. Over the years he'd perfected the art of compartmentalizing his job from his personal life. Normally they never intertwined. Today they overlapped. "Yeah, I'm fine. Look, I'm not going to apologize for what I said. Regardless of what we thought, we are married and today you needed your husband. I would do it all over again if I had to." And he'd keep doing it. For some reason, they'd been given a second chance and he planned to make the most of it. "Come on, let's go in before Italy comes out and asks us why we're sitting in his driveway."

He got out and slammed the car door shut, then strode around the front of the car and grabbed Antonia's door as she opened it. He held out his hand and breathed out when she placed her hand in his. A small show of trust, but he'd take any he could get. He gave it a gentle squeeze before closing her door and pressing the lock button on her key fob.

They'd taken two steps before the front door of the house opened and a whirling dervish disguised as Erin rushed out and grabbed hold of Antonia pulling her into a tight hug, dislodging their joined hands.

"Oh Toni, I've been so scared all day. If Carlos hadn't come home, poor Kieran would've spent the day starving and in a dirty diaper. Why didn't you call me back? I've been an absolute mess." The fear in Erin's voice was plain and he mentally kicked himself for not thinking of sending a message after they'd finished everything, to let the guys know Antonia was all right.

Robot stood back, letting the friends comfort each other in a silent hug. Over the top of their heads, he spied Italy in the doorway arms crossed. He lifted his chin and received one in response.

"How about we go inside," he suggested to the two women.

Erin kept her friend close and Antonia sent him a small smile and mouthed *thank you*. What did she think he'd do? Yank her back in his arms. He wasn't that much of a douche not to know that Erin needed reassurance that nothing was wrong with her friend.

The two women walked inside and as he was about to cross the threshold when Italy stilled his movement.

"You need something?" he asked.

"Truthfully, how is she? She looks fine, but outside appearances can be deceiving."

Robot sighed. "She's holding up really well. But yeah, the shock hit her not long after you guys left and I'm betting it's going to be the same later on. You know how it is."

Normally he pounded the pavement in an attempt to outrun the demons after returning from a mission. Then he'd find himself talking to his commander or one of the shrinks they had on base. He wasn't ashamed to seek help when he needed it and encouraged the other guys on the team to do the same. When they were in the middle of a shit storm the last thing any one of them needed was one of the team losing himself in his head and putting them all in danger. Even though they groused about it all the time, the guys on the team followed orders and talked to professionals when the need arose. That alone was one of the reasons their team was so effective.

"You plan on staying with her tonight?" Italy asked.

"Yep." Robot had a fair idea that when he presented that fact to Antonia she was going to try and fight him, but on this, he wasn't going to budge.

"Good." Italy nodded and then lowered his voice. "Has she forgiven you for blurting out about you guys being—you know." He pointed to his ring finger on his left hand.

"For the moment. I think her mind is full of what she's been through. I'm guessing she'll drag my ass over the coals soon enough."

Italy slapped him on the back, laughing. "That I'd like to see. There's a bit to this story about you guys being married, isn't there?"

"Yep." He didn't want to get into with Italy in the hallway of his house. "Come on, let's see what the girls are doing."

He turned his back on his friend and headed for the living room, the likely place where Antonia and Erin would've headed.

They should've discussed how they were going to broach the subject of their marriage to Erin. He had no idea how she'd react to the news. From the time Erin turned up with Antonia in his backyard over a year ago, he would've had to been blind not to see the closeness of the relationship between the two women. They'd been best friends since high school and probably shared everything. They could have even made some sort of wedding pact like two women associated with Ghost and Truck of the Delta team they'd worked with recently had made.

He and his team had heard all about the four-couple wedding the guys on the Delta team had had from Wolf. Having met both, Truck and Ghost, he was glad it had gone off well.

When he walked into the room, the two girls were deep in conversation, but the connection between him and Antonia tugged at him, pulling him toward her without conscious thought. She lifted her head and locked her gaze with his the second he took his first step into the room.

There was room on her other side on the couch. He acted entirely on instinct and sat next to her, resting his arm across the back of the couch so that his fingertips brushed her shoulder.

A little of his tension dissipated out of him when she leaned into him, and placed a hand on his thigh, her familiar scent of lemon and peppermint swirled around him.

"Okay you guys, what the fuck is going on between the two of you," Erin demanded. "And don't tell me nothing. You two have been playing some sort of cat and mouse game for over a year. Now it looks like the cat has caught the mouse and I want answers."

Antonia looked up at him, panic in her eyes. He squeezed her shoulder in reassurance. Letting her know in that simple touch that, like always, he had her six and they'd face this together.

ANTONIA RECEIVED THE MESSAGE ROBOT WAS transmitting to her—they'd deal with the fallout of their announcement together.

What was going to piss Erin off the most was the fact that Antonia had kept it all a secret in the first place. They always confided in each other.

"Why are you waiting so long to answer me?" Erin asked. "And don't try coming up with some stupid lie. I'm not going to buy it."

As if she'd ever lie to her friend. Choosing not to tell her about being married wasn't the same as lying—was it?

Another squeeze on her shoulder had her looking up at Robot, the question plain to see in his eyes—did she want him to say it? She gave a slight shake of her head. This was her responsibility. She could do it.

Making sure all her attention was focused on the magazines strewn across the coffee table and not on her friend, because if she looked at Erin, she might lose her courage, she took a deep breath and began.

"Robot and I are married." Five little words, seemingly so easy to say, after all. But, like a stone thrown in a pond, the ripples of her declaration could be far reaching. As it was Robot hadn't said how the guys had taken it.

"What?"

Oh, fuck. This wasn't good. Erin's response was quiet and calm, not a screech like she fully expected. Maybe if she said it again, she'd get the reaction she wanted and could deal with.

"Robot and I are married."

Erin shot up from the couch and put some distance between them. For once her life, Antonia wished Carlos was around, but she'd heard the baby cry when Robot appeared in the doorway and figured he was off attending to his son.

"I thought I told you not to lie to me, Toni. So how about you tell me the truth."

Well, this was definitely unexpected. She hadn't thought Erin wouldn't believe her. She pulled away from the warmth of having Robot beside her and walked over to her friend, placing both hands on her shoulder so Erin had no choice but to look up at her.

"I'm telling you the truth, Ren. We're married."

Whether it was the tone of her voice or the fact Erin could see the truth shining in her eyes, her mouth dropped open and she looked between Antonia and where Robot sat on the couch, still and silent.

"Shut. The. Fuck. Up." Then Erin slapped her on the arm. "Why the hell didn't you tell me?"

Now here was the Erin she knew and loved. Without thinking, she pulled her friend into a hug, just needing to know she hadn't ruined their friendship by keeping a secret from her.

"Because I thought it was over and I'd never have to see Robot again." As far as explanations went, it was a pretty pathetic attempt at one.

"Yeah, I don't believe that." Erin looked at her and then over at the man sitting on the couch, observing them both in that freaky SEAL way of his.

The man of the hour stood. "I think, as far as explanations go, we need Italy here, too, so we only have to tell the story once. How about I got get a bottle of wine for you girls and a couple of beers for me and Italy, then we can all sit down and talk about it."

"Stop trying to control every situation," Antonia huffed out. She'd been in charge of her life for a long time, she wasn't going to relinquish control now. He was taking this whole 'still married' thing too far.

This was why their marriage needed to be dissolved as soon as possible, they got on each other's nerves too easily.

And yet you loved having him by your side today.

Today was different, she told the voice in her head. All their interactions since their lives bounced together again had been contentious, to say the least. Robot always making smart-ass comments then she'd bite his head off. If she thought about it too hard, she'd have to admit that his comments weren't that bad. More tongue in cheek, like when they were all waiting for Suzie's baby to be born and he'd whispered in her ear that if things had been different it could've been her giving birth to their child but wasn't it lucky that it wasn't them. She'd called him an asshole, because he had been. It had been like he was giving her a dream and then snatching it away.

Deep down she wanted to have children and for a split second she had imagined what it would've been like if they'd been expectant parents. Her reaction was just because Erin had been pregnant and blissfully happy. Suzie appeared happy with Joker and, yeah, jealousy was a bitch emotion.

The pop of a cork releasing from the neck of wine bottle burst the bubble of her thoughts. So deep in her remunerations she'd missed Robot leaving the room to get the drinks and Carlos walking with in Kieran.

Her eyes were drawn to the little bundle wrapped up in a lime green bunny rug. Although little was an anomaly now. Kieran was getting bigger and bigger with each passing day.

The need to hold him almost overwhelmed her. After the day she'd had, she wanted the comfort holding a new life could bring.

She walked over to where Erin sat. "Can I hold him?" she asked quietly.

Erin handed over the baby without question, as if she instinctively knew this was what Antonia needed.

Kiernan's little face peered up from the blanket, his lips stretching into a gummy grin when he recognized his godmother. "Hey little man, you're getting too handsome for your own good."

He waved his arm as though he agreed with her. She laughed and controlled the shimmy in her stomach when Robot slipped his arm around her waist.

She turned her head to look at the big tough Navy SEAL in time to see his features soften as he reached out and traced a finger down Kieran's perfect chubby baby cheek.

Antonia willed herself to keep rigid and not melt into his side, no matter how much she wanted to. This could almost be like she'd imagined in the hospital waiting room all those months ago. Her and Robot and their child.

She took a step away from his heat and sat on the couch. She really needed to get her shit together. Her emotions had to be running high due to everything she'd been through since this morning. That's the only explanation she'd allow herself for picturing a future with her and Robot.

She needed to try harder *not* to like the guy. Sure, he was sexy as sin and together they set the sheets on fire, but that wasn't the basis of a good relationship.

"You guys wanna explain how you're married?" Erin asked pulling her, once again, from all her internal thoughts. She had to stop being so vague otherwise the story will never be told.

Shifting Kieran to a more comfortable position she took a deep breath. "So, you know in *Friends* when Ross and Rachel got so hammered in Vegas that they got married?" She waited until both Erin and Carlos nodded. "Yeah, well, that's what happened with us. We were wasted, didn't know what we were doing and decided to get married. It was a total mistake."

"Dude, seriously? You, the guy who never makes mistakes, got so drunk you got married in Vegas? I don't believe you didn't know what you were doing?" Carlos stated, staring at his team lead incredulously. "You never fuck up like this. I don't buy it."

"What don't you buy, Italy?" Robot asked, his tone low and expressing no emotion. He didn't even look her way.

"Exactly what I said, you never do anything on a whim. You always know what you're doing. I've seen you pretty wasted, and not once, have you done or thought about doing something like getting married."

A small, traitorous part of Antonia perked up at what Carlos was saying. Sure, she'd been drunk on alcohol, but she'd also been drunk on the man sitting beside her. His masculinity had wrapped itself around her like a warm coat and she'd sunk into it gratefully. All she'd wanted was to be taken and protected by him, so she'd suggested marriage.

On a whim.

On a joke—but really kind of meaning it at the same time.

She'd expected him to run away as fast as he could, instead he'd framed her face, kissed the beejeezus out of her and rushed her to the chapel.

Morning regrets had pummeled her faster than a flying fist of a heavyweight boxer. It had been she who had said the marriage needed to end. Not Robot. He'd lazed in bed, his sexy chest on display with the sheet barely covering him and stared at her while she stuttered through the little speech she'd prepared in the bathroom. Her head was pounding at the time and heart was telling her to leap back into bed and give the marriage a go.

She ignored her heart. Nothing good ever came of

trusting emotions. Her parents' numerous marriages and divorces displayed just how sacred the thought love was to them. She didn't trust the emotion and, while she wished all the people around her who were falling in love well, experience had shown her, when things got tough, everyone ran. Would Robot have run if she hadn't been the one to push for the annulment? Or would he have wanted to see if their spur of the moment marriage would work?

"I knew what I was doing," Robot conceded. "I also knew what I was doing when we agreed to annul the marriage the next morning."

"I didn't think a marriage could be annulled if you'd consummated it?" Erin piped up, her eyes darting from Antonia to Robot. Antonia fought to keep the heat from rising in her face. She knew Erin's question had a hidden depth. Her friend wanted to know if she and Robot had slept together.

Well, yes, they had. On more than one occasion.

Antonia sighed. "You can get a marriage annulled with a variety of reasons, *Want of Understanding* is one."

"Then why are you still married now," Erin asked. Sometimes Antonia loved her friend's bluntness, other times not so much.

"Seems my former lawyer never filed the papers," Robot said. "And before you ask, I don't know why, seeing as I only found out the other day via a voicemail and I haven't had a chance to call him back because I was busy today."

Busy with a murder and the police and her.

"And neither of you thought to check that the marriage was dissolved? Seems like that's something that should've been looked into." This came from Carlos, pulling her out of the whirlpool of anxiety threatening to pull her under, and his suspicious tone annoyed her.

"Robot assured me that once I signed the papers and sent them back, he'd make sure everything was handled on his end and confirm with me when it was all done."

Carlos raised his eyebrow. "Clearly, he didn't."

"Watch it, Italy. I don't like the tone you're taking here. Yes, mistakes were made. I should've followed up, but we went to Afghanistan on that mission that should've been an in and out, but ended up taking far longer than we anticipated. By the time I got back, the last thing I was thinking about was my Vegas marriage."

"What about you, Toni? Didn't you think it strange you hadn't heard from him?" Erin asked.

Antonia shrugged. "I'd lost my phone, remember? I had to get a new number and add back all my contacts, so even if he tried, Robot wouldn't have been able to get hold of me."

God, even to her own ears both their explanations sounded lame, they'd done the right thing and yet to the outside observer they hadn't. She should've been more proactive in making sure the annulment was finalized, but she'd gone with the edict of *what happens in Vegas, stays in Vegas*. The mistake she was better off forgetting.

"Well then, I guess it's lucky neither of you decided to get married in the last couple of years. That would've really been a shitstorm," Erin commented.

"Tell me about it," Antonia muttered. "Although, only knowing him as Robot would've made him difficult to find anyway."

"Dude, you didn't use your name when you said your vows? That's jacked."

Robot tensed beside her and Antonia wasn't sure if he was about to jump up and knock Carlos out. She laid her hand on his him, letting him know she'd take point on this question. "I'm pretty sure he did use his full name, but the wedding is still a blur so I wouldn't have been able to recall his name if I tried." What happened when they got back to their room wasn't something she was likely to forget. Even in her inebriated state, she'd recalled it was the best sex she'd ever had—until the weekend she'd walked into his backyard. The second he spied her he hadn't let her out of his sight. Whatever had pulled them together in Vegas swirled around them the whole day and they'd ended up in bed again. The sex that night was unbelievable. Surprising how being sober can make a huge difference to reactions and experiences.

"Now everything makes sense," Erin mused.

"What do you mean?" asked Antonia.

Her friend smiled slyly. "Well, all the times you guys fought whenever you were within six feet of each other. Toni, the way you would never answer my questions about you and Robot and would always change the subject. They often say there's a fine line between love and hate. I think you two are a good example of that. But I still don't get why you didn't mention the whole Vegas marriage thing."

The baby crying saved her from refuting Erin's assertions or answering why she never mentioned her marriage. She neither loved nor hated Robot. He just created emotions within her she didn't know how to handle, and she didn't like not being in control of herself.

Erin took Keiran from her arms and Antonia leaned back on the couch, closing her eyes to shut everyone and everything out. Not for the first time, she wished for a time machine that would take her back to that night in Vegas and she'd make different decisions. Although, she had a feeling that even if she could do things over, she'd still be drawn to Robot. Whether she'd met him in Vegas or had met him for the first time at the party at his house, there was an innate quality about him the drew her into his orbit. Now that she was in it, she wasn't sure she ever wanted to leave. Yet, she couldn't risk staying. She'd seen how love can turn on a person. The hurt love can bring. Walking away from Robot again was her only option.

CHAPTER 5

All Antonia wanted to do was go home and sleep for two days. The past couple of hours at Erin's place had been intense. Thank goodness Keiran had cried and basically stopped the Spanish Inquisition being conducted by Erin and Carlos. A silent message must have been passed between Robot and Carlos because when Erin returned and went to start in again, Carlos had laid his hand on her arm and looked at her, obviously relaying Robot's message.

She'd told him earlier she didn't want him taking over the situation, but right now she was grateful. She'd spent the whole day talking. Her throat hurt. She was tired and, not that she'd admit it out loud to the man beside her, she was too scared to go back to her apartment.

Realistically, the likelihood of the murderer finding her was pretty slim. Well, at least she hoped it was. All her prayers at the moment were that he hadn't seen her like she'd seen him. But even as she kept saying the silent pleas, the truth knocked at the back of her head—he had as good a view of her as she had of him. Her only hope was, because the complex was large, he would have a lot of difficulty connecting the dots and working out which apartment was hers.

"We're here," Robot said quietly.

Already? Hadn't they just got in the car?

She opened her eyes and saw that instead of being at her apartment complex, they were parked in Robot's driveway.

She sat up a little straighter. "What the hell are we doing here? I thought you were taking me home, Robot."

"For tonight, you are home. I don't think you should be by yourself. It's been a difficult day for you." He reached out and trailed a finger softly down her cheek, and she had to hold herself still to prevent herself from leaning into him. "I have a feeling you don't *want* to be alone either."

Damn the man. How did he know that I was thinking this exact same thing?

Fatigue slammed into her with the force of a freight train. She didn't have the strength to argue with him. And he was right, why fight it?

"I don't have any clothes with me," she murmured.

"Erin packed a bag with some of her things for you. She also threw in a spare toothbrush and some other essentials, was the term I think she used."

Tears threatened to erupt from her again. So many people taking care of her. It was a foreign concept for her. She'd always looked out for herself and when people needed help, she was the first one to put her hand up to help out.

"I didn't see you carrying a bag when we left their place."

"That's because Erin put it in the car a few minutes before we left." He released his seatbelt and opened his door. "Don't move," he commanded and got out.

Antonia sat and tracked his movements around the front of the car then he opened the backdoor behind her and, she assumed, grabbed the bag Erin had packed. In a flash, her door was open and he extended a hand toward her.

She looked at it then up at the man it belonged to. His face was shadowed in the evening light, but his strength couldn't be denied and an overwhelming need to be wrapped up in his strong arms swept over her.

Releasing her own seatbelt, she placed her hand in his. His fingers closed around hers in a sure grip and his warmth spread through her soul. Without thought, she leaned into him and laid her head on his chest.

"Thank you for coming today, Brendan," she said softly.

"Wouldn't be anywhere else, T," he responded and kissed the top of her head. "Let's get you inside and to bed."

She shivered at the thought of bed. Would he put her in one of his guest rooms or would she be sleeping with him? A day ago, she would've balked at the thought of sleeping in the same bed as Robot, but tonight, tonight she wanted it. Wanted to be held in his strong arms. Wanted to know she didn't have to be by herself.

Once inside the house, everything was immediately familiar. Robot's house was always the place where the team met up for various get-togethers. She'd been to the house numerous times and each time the surroundings grew more familiar to her and she normally walked around the house as if she owned it.

Tonight, though, she was nervous about what was going to happen next. This was the first time they'd been by themselves in house since that first weekend over a year ago. Did she go to one of the guest rooms or did she go to Robot's room? Was he expecting more from her tonight than merely sleeping? Did she want more than to sleep tonight?

No. She stomped on that thought of her and Robot making love. God, talk about muddying the waters of their relationship more by having sex. Losing herself in the sensations Robot could generate in her so she could forget all she'd been through was a temptation she couldn't give into. She may feel wonderful afterwards, but it would only complicate their already complicated relationship.

"Why don't you go get ready for bed, I'll be up in a few."

"Which room?" she asked.

Robot closed the small distance between them, the bag dropping from his hand with a thud as it hit the ground. He threaded his fingers through her hair until he cupped her skull. "Mine. But I promise you this, T, nothing will happen. I'm just going to hold you and keep you safe all night. Okay?"

Words were impossible. The ice normally present in

his eyes, had melted giving way to an oasis of blue that she could sink into. “Okay.”

“Good, now.” He bent and picked the bag up. “Here you go. You know which way to go?”

Antonia gripped the bag and nodded. Their eyes remained locked together for a couple of heartbeats before she broke the connection and headed toward his bedroom. If she stayed any closer to him, she couldn't be responsible for her actions. No matter how much her body may want to lose itself his.

The second she walked into his room and saw his bed, she was assailed with a million memories. Even now her stomach churned in excitement and her cheeks began to tingle. She closed her eyes and counted to ten, willing her body to stop this visceral response she fell into every time she was near the man.

“Not tonight, Antonia,” she muttered as she strode over to the bed and dumped the bag on the navy blue comforter.

The room was a typical bachelor's room. A dark mahogany chest of drawers against one wall. Two matching bedside tables next to a large bed. She recalled joking with Robot that his bed was huge, too big for one person. At the time she'd been hit with a stab of jealousy wondering how many other women had shared it, but he told her he'd had it custom-made and it turned out bigger than he anticipated. Getting sheets was a bitch but he managed. He also informed her that the furniture was only a month old and she would be the first person to share it. She'd jumped him them, wanting to test it out.

How many other women had been in that bed since

she'd last lain in it? She quickly pushed the thought away. She didn't want to know.

Determined to be tucked beneath the covers and asleep before Robot walked into the room, she unzipped the bag, rolling her eyes when she spied the box of condoms with a yellow sticky note attached.

Just in case. E

Antonia knew for a fact that Robot had his own supply of condoms in the top drawer of one of the bedside tables. At least, they were there the last time she'd been with him. Where they still there? Or had the box been replaced numerous times over?

Now that the seed had been planted, she couldn't unroot it. But she had to fight the urge to pull open the drawer to see if the same box still resided in it.

Antonia shook her head, couldn't give in. It wasn't her place to know what Robot had done or not done in the last year since they spent the weekend here.

During all the times the team had gotten together, he'd been by himself. He'd always made his way over to her side, to either antagonize her or check to see if she needed anything. Surely if he'd been with someone, Erin would've mentioned it to her.

"Oh my God, what am I doing?" she said out loud trying to shush the calamity of conversation going on in her head. "Just get into bed and forget about everything."

Getting into bed was easy, forgetting about everything else was going to be more difficult. But she could do it. Push everything out of her mind that didn't need to be there—most especially Robot's sex life.

With that resolve thrumming through her, she pulled

out the oversized t-shirt Erin had packed and padded to the bathroom. She looked longingly at the shower. She'd love nothing more than to let warm water sluice over her and wash away the taint of the day. But knowing her, once she got in there, it would be about twenty minutes before she got out again and that was twenty minutes she didn't have.

She quickly washed her face, brushed her teeth and changed in to the t-shirt. Looking in the mirror she rolled her eyes at the shirt Erin had given her. Of course, it was a Navy SEAL shirt, though faded, the trident symbol was obvious.

What would Robot think when he spied her in a shirt that so clearly belonged to Carlos? Would he rip it off her and demand she wear one of his?

She quivered at the thought of standing in just panties in front of him.

Okay, we're still not going there, she admonished her sub-conscious which had turned into a sex-crazed young adult.

Antonia picked up her pile of clothes and walked back into the bedroom, stopping when she spied Robot standing in the middle of the room, shirtless, his impressive chest on display for her to see.

Crap, she'd taken too long and her plan to be fast asleep by the time he walked back in disappeared quicker than a mouse spying a cat.

"Hey, are you doing okay?" he asked when he saw her standing in the doorway.

"Yep." She kept her eyes averted as she went past him to dump her clothes on the bag, which now lay on the floor and not in the middle of the bed where she'd left it.

"What's that shirt you're wearing?" he asked when she straightened up.

Oh boy, here we go, what's going to happen now. She faced him. "Just a shirt Erin put in my bag for me to sleep in."

His eyes narrowed for a second and she waited for the explosion to happen. Instead, his features relaxed and he chuckled. "That asshole. I knew he'd taken my favorite shirt."

So not the reaction she was expecting at all. "What? This is your shirt?" She pointed to the soft material.

"Yeah, it is. Italy kept denying he'd taken it. It's a running joke between the guys in the team. One or the other always takes it. It's been missing for a couple of months now. That asshole is going to pay tomorrow at PT for taking my shit."

"I don't think I'll ever understand you guys. You're grown men, yet you act like a bunch of vagabond teenagers."

He crossed his arms over his chest, drawing her eyes to the way the muscles rippled with the movement. "Vagabond teenagers, huh?"

"Yes." She feigned a yawn, because if she didn't get into bed, she would more than likely wrap her arms around Robot and ask him to kiss away all her pain. "It's been a fucked up kind of day and all I want to do is sleep. I just hope I can."

Immediately the humor left his face and his serious I'm-the-team-lead look returned. "Do you need something to help you sleep? I can give you a sleeping pill, although I'm not sure that's a good idea."

The thought of taking a sleeping pill didn't appeal. No doubt she'd sink into the sweet oblivion of sleep, but it was the waking up that she wouldn't look forward to. She'd heard enough stories from friends to know after they'd taken one, the next day it felt like they were wandering around in a fog.

"Thanks, but no. I'm sure once my head hits the pillow, I'll be out like a light." She crossed her fingers behind her back.

He studied her for a few moments longer and she lifted her chin and met his gaze. A silent battle of the wills took place, before he shook his head. "Fine. Get into bed, I'm just going to...yeah." He brushed past her and out the room.

"What the hell was that all about?" she murmured to the empty room.

Giving up trying to understand what was going through Robot's head, she climbed into bed. Immediately her senses were assailed with the scent of the aftershave he wore. The cool, crisp scent reminded her of fall nights in upstate New York. A hint of pine in the air and the crunch of early fresh snow under her feet. She'd only been upstate once with an old college boyfriend, but the memory had stuck with her. Not the boyfriend, he'd turned out to be a total dick, but memories of the lodge they'd stayed at and the surrounding wooded area, had made a lasting impression.

She tucked that memory close to her mind as she shut her eyes and willed sleep to come quickly.

ROBOT PLACED THE GLASS IN THE SINK AND GAZED OUT AT his darkened backyard. He had to walk out of his bedroom otherwise he would've forgotten all his good intentions and scooped Antonia up in his arms and kissed her senseless.

Seeing her in his favorite t-shirt, the fabric skimming the middle of her thighs, had been temptation personified. Then he took in her face, surrounded by a gorgeous mass of curls, and the vulnerability he saw struck him deep in the heart. He wanted to wrap her in his arms and never let her go. He wanted to kiss her and make love to her until all her fears and doubts were gone. Only the faint hint of purple beneath her eyes had stopped him from following through with his actions.

Instead, he'd stumbled over his words like a teenage boy and bolted from the bedroom. If the guys could have seen him, they would've laughed their heads off. He was always cool and calm. He might have gotten his nickname because he could do a mean robot dance, but over time his lack of emotion and reaction in certain situations had other teams wondering if he'd gotten the name because of his robot-like nature. He let them believe that.

He transferred his gaze from the yard to the glowing numbers on his microwave. Forty-five minutes had passed since he'd walked out of his bedroom. Plenty of time for Antonia to fall asleep. At least he hoped so, after the trauma she'd seen he wouldn't be surprised if she tossed and turned all night. He planned to be right by her side should she have a nightmare.

Which she could be having right now.

The inner thought spurred him into action and he strode back through the house to his room. The lamp on his side table cast a golden glow around the room. Antonia was curled up on his side of the bed. One hand under the pillow while the other was on top of the covers. She appeared to be sleeping the sleep of the dreamless and he was glad for that.

Damn, she looked perfect in his bed.

He'd keep her there if she'd let him, but that would never happen. Come tomorrow, in the cold light of day, she'd demand he drive her home then they'd argue about it, but in the end he'd heed her wishes, even though it went against everything in him to do so. As much as he wanted to protect and guard her, he wouldn't force the issue, but he'd be close by if she needed him. He would make sure she understood that.

Making as little noise as possible he took care of the necessities and then shucked his jeans and boxers. Going over to his dresser, he pulled out a pair of gym shorts and thrust his legs into them. Normally, he slept naked but didn't think Antonia would appreciate it if she woke up during the night and found him sans clothes. The shorts would have to do, even if he didn't like sleeping with the restrictions of clothing when he was home. After so many nights sleeping on hard packed earth in his full kit, he liked the freedom sleeping nude gave him.

Did Antonia sleep naked as well?

His dick sprang to life at the thought and he cursed himself for having a thought like that as he was about to climb into bed with her.

He willed his engorged flesh to cease and desist, while he lifted the covers and slid between the cool sheets. It felt weird as hell to be sleeping on this side of the bed, but he had no plans to disturb the sleeping woman next to him. Her soft exhales of breath were reassuring that no demons had decided to threaten her in her sleep. He turned onto his side so that he could look at her and confirm that she was truly asleep. Her eyelashes rested in half-moons against her sleep pinkened cheeks. Her mouth was slightly open, and her fingers twitched every now and then. He could watch her sleep for eternity. Never one to believe in fate, hell, he walked into situations fate ran away from, but Antonia turning up in his life out of the blue and now this marriage issue, he couldn't help but think he was being sent a message. He hadn't looked at another woman since that night in Vegas. He would do everything possible to convince her to give their marriage a second chance.

He didn't want to let Antonia go.

CHAPTER 6

A GROAN WOKE Antonia from her dreamless sleep. For a few seconds she felt disoriented not recognizing where she was. Nor recognizing the sound. She was pretty sure it hadn't been she who'd groaned.

"Get him." The words were mumbled next to her, and everything came rushing back in a flood. Her heart went from zero to sixty and her lips went drier than a desert.

She'd witnessed a murder.

Had to explain her marriage to their friends.

Currently sleeping in Robot's bed.

Oh my God. She turned on her side to look at the man. Even though the light was switched off, the faint glow from the moon filtered through the curtainless windows. Robot's brow was furrowed, and she could see a sheen of sweat across his forehead.

"You can't let him get her. We have to save her." Anguish colored his words. His legs moved restlessly beneath the covers, tugging them away from her body.

"I've got to get to her. I've got to get her." He repeated the litany over and over.

Anxiety built inside of her and she reached out a hand to touch his shoulder, only to pull back at the last second.

Should I wake him?

It wasn't hard to work out he was in the throes of a nightmare. The irony of the situation wasn't lost on her. If anyone should be having a nightmare right now, it should be her.

Had helping her triggered Robot's own forgotten memories? He kept mumbling about needing to save a woman, his words sometime slurred, sometime shouted. Was this woman from one of the missions? She was aware, from talking to Erin, that the team members never talked to their spouses or girlfriends about what they did, or had to do, when they were away. Most of the missions were top secret and under the radar kind of stuff.

"Oh my God, no. Fuck no. No. No. No."

Fear now gripped Antonia, twisting her insides into a mass of knots, seeing her big brave SEAL in such distress. His hands were now twisting the covers and she was surprised the fabric hadn't ripped with the force of his motions.

She had to wake him. But she had to do it carefully.

Once again, she reached out to touch him gently on the shoulder freezing when he sat upright, his eyes still firmly shut.

"No. Antonia. Nooooooo." His cry echoed around the room.

What the hell?

He was dreaming about her?

Throwing caution to the wind and disregarding the possibility that she might get hurt she wrapped her hand around his bicep, the muscle tense and hard as granite beneath her fingers.

"Brendan. Wake up."

He didn't wake but brought his hands up to cover his face. "No, I can't lose you," he whispered.

God, she wanted to cry at the agony etched over his face and in every taut muscle of his body. She had to wake him. Bring him out of the well of pain he swam in.

"Robot," she said a little louder and shook him gently. "Wake up. You're dreaming."

It was enough. His eyes shot open and he jerked his head to face her. His gaze locked on her, but he wasn't really seeing her. His chest heaved with every breath he took. "Antonia?"

"Yeah, I'm here. You were dreaming."

In a blur of movement, she was hauled against his chest and his hands framed her face. "You're here." He repeated before his mouth crashed over hers. This wasn't a lustful kiss; it was a kiss of desperation, impossible to ignore and so she opened her mouth and allowed him access.

The arms that had held in her a breathtakingly tight embrace loosened a fraction as his kiss slowed.

When the need to breath took over them, his lips peppered over her face.

"I." Kiss

"Thought." Kiss

"You." Kiss

"Were gone." Kiss

This wasn't the man she'd known over the last year. That man was strong and never let anything bother him. This man was still caught in the remnants of his dream and she wasn't sure how he'd react if he was fully aware of what he was doing. How he was acting. And what he was saying.

He laid back down, keeping her firmly entrenched in his arms. His head resting in the crook where her neck met her shoulder. "I thought I'd lost you," he whispered. "I couldn't bear that."

The tension leeched out of him and she lifted her head to see that he appeared to have fallen back asleep. His brow had smoothed out and so had his breathing. When she went to move, his arms tightened.

Okay then, he wasn't going to let her go, and if she was being honest with herself, she didn't want to move from his embrace. A yawn wracked her body and her eyelids grew heavy. She'd rest her eyes for a moment, let him fall into a deeper sleep then she'd move so they both could sleep more comfortably.

Yes, that was a good plan.

THE FAINT RINGING OF A PHONE INTERRUPTED ANTONIA'S sleep. She blinked a couple of times, before closing her eyes again, reaching out to see if her phone was on the side table.

Her hand connected with the hard planes of flesh instead. Before she could move, a large warm hand closed over hers, locking it into place.

"They'll call back if it's important." A sexy, gruff sleep-laden voice grumbled beside her.

Robot.

Clearly, he recognized her ring tone. She imagined if it was his phone, he'd have sprung out of bed at the first sound.

She opened her eyes to find his head turned to the side, watching her closely. "Morning," she mumbled.

"Morning. How did you sleep? Any dreams?"

Antonia propped herself up on her elbow, finding his question interesting, considering it had been he who had the dreams and not she.

Did he not remember his nightmare?

His desperation at finding her beside him and not lost to him?

He really didn't recall?

"No. No dreams," she said cautiously. "How did you sleep? Did you have any dreams?"

A flash of emotion flared in his eyes and his gaze darted away from hers. "No. No dreams."

Hmm, interesting, trying to avoid acknowledging he'd had a nightmare—typical male. Never wanting to admit he was vulnerable. Especially when he was Navy SEAL, the toughest of the toughest. No doubt, in his mind, he wasn't allowed to show any weakness.

He loosened his hold on her hand and she tapped her fingers on his warm, bare chest. "I think you lie, Brendan "Robot" Dean."

A sigh rippled through him, and she held her breath, waiting to see what he did next.

"Why do you say that?" he asked cautiously.

Did she push it? In her mind, it was clear he recalled having the dream, but he didn't want to talk about it. For some reason that cut deep. If the roles were reversed, he'd expect her to talk about it and share it with him. Why couldn't he do that with her?

On the other hand, did she want to start the day out with an argument? Because if she pushed him on the subject, a disagreement between them was as likely as the sun rising in the east. Wanting to keep the unlikely peace that had sprung up between them, she let it go. "No reason." She tossed the covers back and scooted out of the bed. "I'm going to take a shower. I need to go back to my place and get ready for work."

"Do you think it's wise to go back after yesterday?"

She placed her hands on her hips, trying to ignore his autocratic tone. "Are you talking about my apartment or work?"

"Both."

"I can't take any more time off work and I'm not going to let some loser keep me away from my apartment."

"That *loser* is a murderer," he responded drily.

Like she needed reminding, she didn't think she'd ever forget the glint of sunlight on the blade. But she'd meant what she'd said. That guy wasn't going to keep out of her home. Plus, she wanted to put space between her and Robot. Sleeping beside him had been wonderful and she hadn't missed his morning erection. A normal male reaction, but feeling the hard length of him against her thigh had caused a million memories to bombard her brain. Being strong and not succumbing to the temptation that was Brendan Dean was proving harder than she'd like to admit.

"I don't need reminding what he is. And you don't get any say in what I do. I'm going to shower, and when I'm dressed, you're going to drive me home then I'm going to work." She glanced at the clock on the side table. "Shouldn't you be at PT now? You mentioned last night you were going to give Carlos a hard time about the t-shirt."

He shrugged. "Yeah, I was, but I'm not now. The guys won't expect me and I'm sure Italy filled them all in on what happened. I'll do double tomorrow and make Italy do triple."

Somehow, she didn't doubt his words about doing twice as much tomorrow to make up for what he missed this morning. She chewed her bottom lip as another thought hit her. "I forgot everyone knows we're married."

"Yep."

His one word response was very helpful—not. "I guess they'll have to get used to the idea that we won't be married for long. I'll call a lawyer today to see what we can do about getting an annulment…or whatever we may need to do now seeing as it's been a couple of years since the initial marriage."

Robot's lips firmed. "We'll sort that out later. My priority is ensuring your safety."

God dammit why did she have to bring up their marriage again? If she hadn't mentioned it, he probably wouldn't have gone all alpha male on her.

Life had become too complicated for her to face at the moment. "Whatever, but I *am* going home, and I *am* going to work. If you choose not to drive me home then that's fine, I'll arrange an Uber." She lifted her chin, gathering up her clothes and letting him know the discussion was over as far as she was concerned.

"Fine. You win."

His lips continued to move, but she couldn't make out what he said. She had a feeling it was *this time.*

Whether it was a one off victory or a final one, she wasn't going to argue. Once she got home, everything would make sense and she could deal with whatever was going to happen next.

THE SECOND THE DOOR CLICKED SHUT TO HIS ENSUITE bathroom, Robot tossed the covers back and slung his legs over the side of the bed, fingers digging into his thighs as his head hung low.

Memories of his dream still lingered in his mind when Antonia's phone woke them. Even now, his breathing became ragged and his heartbeat kicked up a notch or two.

The sound of the water running in the bathroom reassured him that Antonia was safe in his house, but in his dream she'd been taken from him. Kidnapped by a faceless man. When he and the team had found them, the guy's features had transformed into Bryan, Erin's ex-mob boyfriend. He'd smiled evilly as he glared at Robot then shot Antonia in the head.

Agitation built in him and he jumped up from the bed and raced down to his home gym in the basement and slammed his fists repeatedly into the punching bag. He didn't know how long he'd been at it, but when the red haze finally lifted, his body was drenched with sweat and his knuckles were bright red.

"Do you feel better now?"

He whirled around and saw Antonia standing at the top of the stairs, wearing black leggings and an oversized sweater. She looked casually sexy and if he didn't stink to high-heaven he'd drag her body close and lose the lingering fear buried deep in her body.

"How long have you been there?" he asked as he walked over to the small stack of towels. Picking one up, he wiped it over his face and body.

"Long enough to know that was some demon you were fighting. Want to talk about it?"

Robot knew Antonia was referring to the nightmare. She'd eluded to knowing about it this morning and he now remembered waking up and kissing her senseless. But telling her the details wasn't going to happen. She had enough on her plate as it was without having to listen to him.

"Nope." He dropped the towel in the small hamper and strode toward the stairs. "Give me ten minutes and we'll be out of here."

He brushed past her, knowing it was rude and his asshole scale was hitting ten, but he didn't care. Maybe Antonia was right. Maybe they should end this marriage and go about their lives as if it had never happened.

He choked on the thought of not having Antonia in his life. If only he hadn't had that dream last night, then he wouldn't feel this need to lock her away in his house to keep her safe and away from danger.

Shucking his shorts, he strode into the bathroom, flicked the water on and stood under the spray. The cold water stung like a million pinpricks, but he welcomed the sensation. It reminded him of freezing his ass off in the Pacific Ocean as rain pelted him and his team while wave after wave crashed over them during BUD/s training.

There was a reason he'd remained single for most of his life. Relationships were complicated enough, but factor in his job, and it was near impossible to sustain one.

If he had to do it, he'd give Antonia whatever she wanted, an annulment or a divorce. When she found someone else and brought him around the team get-togethers, he'd face it like the sailor he was.

Letting her go would be the best thing for all of them.

Mind made up he turned the dial to hot and soaped himself up, ignoring the ache in the region of his heart.

CHAPTER 7

Ever since she'd spoken to him in his basement, where he'd been pummeling the shit out of a punching bag, Robot had been unusually quiet. What was even more disturbing was the fact that he hadn't even attempted to touch her.

He'd opened doors for her, but he didn't put his hand on the small of her back or touch her cheek like he usually did. Instead, he'd remained resolute and kept his gaze fixed out the windshield.

Any time she'd tried to start a conversation he'd responded with a grunt so she'd given up on that, too.

Now they were only a couple of miles from her apartment and nerves fired up inside her like dry grass when struck with a match. She clasped her fingers together to prevent them from shaking.

I can do this.

I can do this.

She kept chanting the mantra in her mind as they

drove into the complex. Robot rolled down his window and entered the combination to open the gate. As the long metal structure lumbered open, Antonia fought the desire to blurt out that she wanted to go back to Robot's place. A place where she'd felt safe and secure. Any feelings of security she'd had living in her complex died the second she'd witnessed the murder and she didn't realize that fully until this moment. She hadn't expected to feel a fear so intense she thought she was going to throw up.

"Are you okay?" he asked, and she almost celebrated he'd done more than grunt at her.

If she told him she couldn't do this he'd take her back to his place, no questions asked. If it had been the before-the-shower-Robot sitting beside her and not the after-shower-Robot she'd do it. She'd let him know her fears and ask for him to protect her.

Summoning up courage she really didn't feel, she faced him. "I'm fine. Anxious to get to my place. I know that once I'm around my own things, everything will return to normal."

Yeah, keep telling yourself over and over and eventually you might believe it.

That voice really needed to go on a long vacation.

Robot pulled into the visitor's spot assigned to her apartment and switched the car off. "I can take you to Erin's if you want. I know she wouldn't mind if you stayed there a few days."

Wow, what the hell had happened to him in the shower? If she didn't know better, she'd swear that the Robot she'd slept next to, the one who'd clung to her tightly after his dream...

The dream.

Could it be? Had he remembered he'd dreamt something bad had happened to her. Did he think by putting distance between them that it would keep her safe?

Why the hell was she mentally arguing with herself about it. She was getting what she wanted, space from the man. She should be ecstatic about it all.

If the circumstances had been different, then, yeah, she'd be happy. But, as much as she hated to admit it, she needed him.

"I'm surprised you'd palm me off to Erin when last night you were determined to keep me close to you."

He shifted in his seat. "That was last night. Now do you want me to walk you up or are you happy to go up yourself?"

His change of attitude was like a punch to the stomach and a puff of breath burst out of her. This was why she didn't believe in love. "Nice to see you back, the Robot I know so well. And no, I don't need you to see me up to my place. I can do it myself." She opened the door and got out, turning to lean down and look back at him. He still sat rigid in his chair, his expression blank. "I'll get in touch with a lawyer. The sooner this marriage is over the better. Bye *Brendan.*"

Antonia slammed the door and hurried away, not wanting him to see the tears that welled up in her eyes.

The sound of a car door shutting vaguely registered, but her focus was getting to her apartment as soon as possible. She reached the stairs that would take her up to the second floor when an arm hooked around her waist and lifted her off her feet. She yelped and latched onto the only solid thing she could find as she was whirled around—Robot's shoulders.

"T, I'm so sorry." He buried his face into her neck. "You're right, I'm being an asshole."

Without giving her a chance to respond, his lips found hers and she melted into his embrace. Her response to his touch was automatic, when she should've pushed him away. But she needed this connection with him. At this moment in time knowing Robot was her husband and there when she needed him comforted her more than she wanted to admit.

His lips trailed a line along her jaw until he reached her ear. "I shouldn't have pushed you away."

"Yeah, why did you? You've been doing nothing but pull me toward you. If anyone should've been pushing anyone away, it should've been me."

He ran a hand over his head. "I know. We need to talk, but not here?"

Robot slipped an arm around her waist and together they walked up to her apartment. She didn't fight him when he took the keys from her. There was no point, this was a SEAL thing he and the rest of the guys did. Erin had groused about it just after she moved in with Carlos, secretly though Antonia suspected she loved it. Brielle relayed a similar story.

Standing so close to him, she couldn't miss the tensing of his muscles as he flung the door open. "What's wrong?" she whispered and tried to look around his broad shoulders.

"Nothing. Stay behind me while I check the place out."

At least he didn't tell her to wait outside. As they made

their way through her apartment, she felt like she was in a bad detective movie.

"This is probably totally unnecessary. The lock didn't show any signs of forced entry."

"You can never be too careful. You have outside access, they could've come in through the sliding door and you'd never know."

That wasn't very comforting, she hadn't thought about being vulnerable because of her balcony. She supposed he had a point to check it out, not that she'd admit that to him.

"All clear," he said unnecessarily when they returned to the living room.

"Well, that's a relief," she returned barely keeping the sarcasm out of her tone.

He turned. "Yeah it is."

Okay, he was back to being semi-assholeish, not that she didn't deserve it, she wasn't exactly being friendly.

"I've fifteen minutes before I have to leave and go to work. Do you want to explain what all that was downstairs?"

He sighed and in that short huff of breath she could hear a wealth of frustration. How did he do that?

She'd love to have that ability when some of her work-mates annoyed her. Not that it happened often. She loved her job and was lucky to have found it so quickly after moving to Virginia. Part of her wondered if the mysterious Tex, who'd helped the team find her and Erin when Bryan and taken them, had helped her somehow. Apparently, the man could work miracles, but she didn't think he was that good in enabling her to get her job.

Silence stretched between them and her tension level inched up the scale until it was getting close to being in the red zone.

"Time's a wastin', Robot. Start talking or…" The rest of her sentence lodged in her throat when his hands curled over her shoulders. He moved faster than a gazelle fleeing a lion.

"Or what?"

Her insides melted at the authority of his tone. The man infuriated and turned her on all at the same time. How did he do that?

"I'll kick you out?" Way to sound confident and strong.

He chuckled and pulled her close until he held her loosely in his embrace. "Are you saying you'll do it or asking if you can?"

"Semantics." She fluttered her hand in the air.

Another puff of air tickled her neck and he dragged over to the couch with him. "I, um." He paused. "Well, I..." He stopped again.

Antonia disentangled herself from his hold and put some distance between them on the couch. "Is it really this hard to talk to me, Robot? I am your *wife,* you know."

If he wasn't speechless before, he was definitely speechless now and it was almost comical the way his eyes widened and his mouth dropped open. An instant later he'd gathered his composure and the glimpse of a man she was sure no one ever saw, disappeared. "Do you know that's the first time you've said you're my wife?"

She allowed herself a small grin. "It looks like it unlocked the speaker's block you were having. So, how about you ride that pony all the way home."

"Where the hell are you getting these analogies from?"

She shrugged. Words were popping in her mind and she was blurting them out. Not something she normally did. It was common knowledge among the group that she had a blunt tongue, pointing out what others mentally thought but were too polite to say.

"You're still avoiding the subject."

"Fine." He shot up from the couch and began pacing around her small living room. "I had a dream you were taken and sh—I didn't like it."

She gathered that much from his cries when he'd been in the throes of his dream. But had he been about to say that she'd been shot? A shiver rippled down her spine at the thought. When Bryan had taken her and Erin, he'd held them both at gunpoint and it had been the most frightening thing she'd ever experienced. One she didn't what to ever have again.

For supposedly being a cool Navy SEAL, Robot was displaying none of that coolness right now. His steps were jerky and he kept thrusting his hands in and out of his jeans pocket.

Why did the thought of her being hurt and taken distress him so much?

Could he possibly—*no so not going there.*

She jerked her thoughts back from the track they were hurtling down. Nothing came of making assumptions, and she was on her way to making a huge one.

What she could do, was ease his agitation.

She went over to him, halting his pacing. "It was just a dream, Brendan," she said softly. "Dreams don't come true and I'm standing right here in front of you."

"Yeah, you are."

They stood there gazing at each other, his blue eyes mesmerizing her with their intensity. Without even being aware of what she was doing, her reach out and cupped his cheek, the bristles tickling her palm. "Right here," she said again as she went up on tiptoe and pressed her lips against his.

Kissing him could easily be a habit she could fall into. The whole team knew about their marriage now so all her efforts to keep him at a distance in effort to not give away their past knowledge of each other wasn't needed anymore.

She was free to touch him. Kiss him. Hug him, whenever she wanted.

I thought you were going to speak to a lawyer?

Her subconscious taunted her but she ignored it. All that mattered now was reassuring Robot it was just a dream and whatever he'd seen hadn't occurred.

She pressed her body closer to his, his arousal pressed against her stomach and a rush of heat coalesced between her thighs.

"Damn," she muttered as she broke the kiss.

"What?" he asked as he nuzzled her neck with his nose before kissing it, causing more ripples of desire to course through her.

"I really have to go to work and so do you." She pushed against his shoulders and with one last nip at her neck he released his hold. Immediately, she wrapped her arms around herself to hold his heat within her.

"Can I drive you to work?" he asked rubbing the back of his neck.

"No, it's fine, but thank you."

"Right. Well, I'll wait and follow you."

Geez, they'd gone from kissing passionately to having a conversation that could've been between two strangers. "My work is in the opposite direction of the base. I don't need an escort, Robot. Thank you, but I will be okay."

He looked like he was going to argue but she placed her fingers on his lips. "Seriously. I will be okay. But I'll text you when I leave here and when I get to work. How about that?"

"You can text me when you get to work, but I'll leave when you leave."

Okay, she could live with that, and her anxiousness that he'd keep pushing alleviated a little. Who knew compromising could be so easy? Although, not all situations were going to be as smooth to sort out like this one. "That works. I'll be back in ten."

She raced off to her bedroom, she was going to be late, but hopefully work would understand. They'd told her yesterday to take as much time as she needed, but one day off was enough. If she didn't keep busy, she'd remember, and she'd rather not recall what she'd seen. Hopefully with the brief description she'd given the cops yesterday and maybe there was video footage from building security, the perpetrator would be caught, and her life could go on as normal. Question was, did her normal include Robot or not?

More to the point: was she going to end her marriage to him or was she going to try and make it work?

CHAPTER 8

ROBOT PAUSED OUTSIDE of the one meeting rooms on base, he could hear the low hum of the conversation the guys were having. He'd just come from Commander Black's office, explaining all he knew about the situation he'd gone through with Antonia the day before. He also asked for the necessary paperwork to amend his next-of-kin.

The sheets burned a hole in his back pocket. Was he really going ahead with it? Was there any point? He and Antonia still hadn't discussed how they were going to move forward with their marriage.

"Fuck," he muttered, so many unanswered questions. He liked to think with the way she'd compromised with him about letting him know she got to work safely, that thoughts of her contacting a lawyer had disappeared, or at least were beginning to. He wouldn't know unless he asked her, which he planned to do tonight when he arrived at her place after he finished work.

He straightened his shoulders and took a fortifying

breath before he stepped into the conference room. He'd withstood and survived being tortured, he could surely deal with barrage of questions the guys planned to throw at him concerning his marriage.

He pushed the partially closed door open and strode in. Italy was the first to notice him. Then one by one the rest of the guys looked over.

"I suppose you all have questions?" Heading them off before they could strike was a good battle plan, and one they'd used on many occasions.

Joker nodded, a wry smile on his face. "If Emma hadn't been fussing last night, I'm pretty sure Suzie would've made me take her over to Italy's place once she heard you guys were there."

"Thank goodness for fractious babies," Robot responded before pulling out a chair.

"Did you really do a Ross and Rachel from *Friends*?" asked Red.

First Antonia, and now Red, referring to an episode of a show he'd never seen. From the description gave the previous evening, it sounded pretty accurate. "I'm surprised you know about that show, Red."

The other man laughed. "One of my sister's best friends is a screenwriter, she and Jenny would watch that show over and over and sometimes I watched it with them."

"Oh? Is that the chick who was texting you at T-Rex and Brielle's party the other day? The one you insist you're *just friends* with." Cowboy teased while using air quotes.

"Did you just air quote me?" Red asked.

"Correct. Is she one and the same girl," Cowboy persisted, and Robot was glad the heat was off him.

"It's the same person and she's my sister's best friend. I've known her most of my life." He shrugged, but Robot noted he didn't look directly at any of the guys.

"Well, you know what they say," T-Rex teased.

"They say never tap your sister's friend," Red responded. "And this isn't about me, it's about Robot and the fact he's *married* to Antonia."

Shit, he'd thought for sure the guys would continue to razz Red, but he supposed they deserved an explanation. These men were brothers to him. The shit they'd been through together forged a connection that was stronger than blood.

He drummed his fingers on the table. If he kept everything short, concise and to the point, it should keep the questions about his marriage to a minimum. "Yes, Antonia and I got married two years ago. Yes, it was in Vegas. Yes, we'd had a lot to drink. Yes, in the morning we decided to end it. Yes, my former lawyer fucked up and didn't file the papers, so we're still married. As to why I didn't mention it, recall former point about lawyer. Anything else?"

"Notice he didn't say anything about going to a lawyer now to end it." Joker threw into the small silence that had settled over the group.

"He didn't, did he?" said Cowboy.

"What I want to know is..." Interjected Italy who'd been sitting back and not saying a word.

Robot had a feeling he wasn't going to like what Italy was about to say next. He crossed his arms and raised his eyebrow in query.

"Who asked who to get married?" Italy sat back, a smug little smile on his face.

Of course, that would be the question his friend would ask. "It was a mutual decision."

He wasn't lying with his answer. The scene replayed in his mind.

They'd left the casino and were walking down the hallway when he pulled her in tight to avoid a group of people, including a woman wearing a wedding dress. He looked down at Antonia as she looked up at him. He had no idea who moved first, but they exchanged the hottest kiss he'd ever experienced.

A guy staggering behind the group, saw them and joked that the wedding chapel was just down the hall and they should go make it official.

They'd laughed at his suggestion, but the idea wasn't that abhorrent to him. For a guy who liked his life in order, not to mention extremely meticulous in planning his team's missions, the fact he considered marrying to a woman he'd known only a few hours and kissed once, was completely out of character.

Then Antonia had said, *I always loved the idea of a Vegas wedding*. It had sealed the deal and so he got down one on knee and asked her to marry him. She laughed and surprisingly said yes. Twenty minutes later, she sported a diamond solitaire engagement ring, with accompanying filigree wedding band, and he wore a matching band. The chapel had everything they needed.

When he woke the next morning, she was standing by the bed, rings off and holding them out to him. He'd agreed to what she wanted, even though part of him wanted to try and suggest they make it work, but he hadn't told her what he did for a living. Considering how dangerous his job was, ending the marriage seemed the best way to go.

He still had the rings, tucked away in the bottom drawer of his dresser.

A clap on his shoulder brought him out of his memory daze. He looked to his left and spied Italy standing there. "You all right?" he asked.

"Yeah, why wouldn't I be?"

"You've been standing there for the last five minutes looking at the far corner of the room while everyone else has bugged out."

"I was just remembering," he said quietly, as he took in the empty room.

Italy's eyes widened as if surprised Robot would admit something so personal out loud. Hell, he was too, but it was out there, and he didn't care. "You remember the night clearly?"

Robot scrubbed a hand down his face. "I do, and I'm pretty sure Antonia does as well. We were drunk, but as you know, even drunk, some things stick in your mind. How we got married is one of them." He definitely wasn't going to mention he remembered how hot the sex between him and Antonia was, and he was grateful his mind hadn't blocked that out. It was still the best night of his life. Closely followed by the weekend they'd spent at his place when Erin and Antonia first came to town.

Fuck, he was really losing it.

"I think there's a reason why you don't seem angry at your former lawyer," Italy said.

"Oh really, why is that?"

"You want to stay married to Antonia. I'd even go so far as to say that you have feelings for her. You're a guy who doesn't do spontaneous things so for you to get married on whim, she had to have struck something in you. Question is, how does Antonia feel?"

Out of all the guys on the team, he was closest to Italy. They'd saved each other's asses on more than one occasion. Normally, he wasn't one to share his inner thoughts with anyone, but Italy had gone to school with Erin and Antonia. He knew her well, just like he knew Robot.

"I don't know how she feels. She was talking about contacting a lawyer this morning after I'd pissed her off."

"Fuck, dude, you two are always sparking off each other. Erin was right last night, you two are perfect together."

"When did she say that?" Robot recalled most of their conversation and he was pretty sure Erin didn't say that in front of him and Antonia. If she did, both of them would've denied it. Well he would've done so anyway.

"After you'd gone. We were talking about you two, your Vegas marriage, and how you've been acting since she arrived back in your life. Erin's convinced you both secretly love each other but are too stubborn to admit it. Not to mention, she's excited you and Antonia are hitched."

Deep down he was beginning to believe his feelings for Antonia had strengthened and solidified in him, but like hell he'd been shouting it out loud of all to hear.

"Of course, she is. Your woman is nothing but a romantic since the two of you hooked up again."

Italy smiled smugly. "What can I say, I'm her Romeo and she's my Juliet."

Robot faked gag. "That deserves an extra hundred push-ups tomorrow during PT."

Italy punched him in the arm. "Seeing as you have to do an extra one-fifty for missing two days of PT then you can keep me company."

"Robot, Italy, grab the rest of your team and get in my office now. We've got a situation." Commander Black's voice boomed into the room and any humor lingering in Robot drained out. That tone could only mean one thing —they were going to be wheels up in about thirty minutes.

PULLING INTO ERIN'S DRIVEWAY, ANTONIA NOTICED TWO other cars already there. She'd resisted the urge to drive a little further down the street to Robot's house. The guy wasn't there, but he'd called her to tell her they were leaving on a mission and he didn't know how long they'd be.

Two minutes later, Erin had called her and told her, in no uncertain terms, she expected Antonia at her place after work for the usual girls' night they had when the guys went on a mission.

Normally, she was the extra, the one not associated with anyone on the team, but now she was very much one of them. She was Robot's wife.

Unconsciously, she rubbed her ring finger on her left hand. The rings he'd chosen for her had been beautiful and she remembered tearing up when he slipped them on her finger. At the time she'd blamed the alcohol, but now she wondered how it was possible to feel such emotion with a guy she'd only just met. Was she the same as her parents? Always falling in love in an instant, only to find out later it wasn't love at all, but infatuation? Was what she was feeling for Robot only infatuation though? Could what they had be different to what her parents had with each other?

"Not going there, Antonia. Not going there," she muttered to herself as she opened the car door. She was a little late since she was held up at work, but no doubt, the girls had gossiped about her and Robot's marriage and had a list of questions ready to fire her way.

She hoped to God, Erin had a good supply of wine. Antonia had an idea she would need the fortification of a good white to get her through this evening.

Her cell phone buzzed in her bag, probably Erin wondering where she was. She dug the device out of the depths of her purse. The number flashing up wasn't one she recognized and normally she'd send it to voice mail, but now things were different. Robot had left to go on a mission, but it was possible he could be calling her. Not that she expected him to, but occasionally Carlos would call Erin.

She swiped to accept. "Hello."

"Bitch, you better keep your mouth shut or you'll pay." Spit out a deep, harsh voice.

The call disconnected before she could say anything. Shock rooted her to the spot. Blood rushed through her system, pounding in her ears as her heart thudded rapidly in her chest.

That wasn't…

It couldn't be.

She shouldn't be here. If they had her number, they could trace her to Erin's place then everyone would be in danger. She couldn't put the girls at risk.

"Toni, are you gonna stand out there all night? Get your butt inside."

Antonia looked up and saw Erin standing in the doorway. Fuck, what was she going to do and why did the call have to happen when Robot had just left on a mission?

Her phone rang again in her hand, but she ignored it. She didn't want to pick it up in case it was another threatening call. The ringing stopped, and she breathed out in relief.

Okay, now she could think and come up with a plan to keep everyone safe. She just needed to feign some sort of sickness. With two young babies in the house, neither mother would want their child to get sick. Then she could go home

No. Not home. She wouldn't be safe there.

A hotel.

Yes, a hotel was the perfect place. She didn't care how much she'd have to pay for a room, it was worth it if it meant keeping Erin and the others safe. Brielle didn't need to be embroiled in another drama. She was still recovering from being kidnapped twice. Once by herself and the other time with T-Rex.

She looked up again, Erin had her hands on her hips now, a sure sign she was getting pissed off. Plastering a smile—oh no, no smile, she was faking being sick, she needed to look miserable.

Her phone started ringing again.

Fuck.

She hit decline and squeezed her fingers tighter around the electronic device.

Taking her time, she stood a few feet away from Erin, hoping her friend couldn't see the look of distress on her face.

"Hey E, I'm gonna have to bail on tonight."

Erin's eyes narrowed. "Why?"

"I almost threw up twice on the way over. I must be coming down with the bug that's going around the office. I don't want to make Kieran or Emma sick. I think it's best I go home."

"Are you really sick or just faking it because you know we're going to ask a million questions?"

She knew Erin would think it's an excuse, but she couldn't crumple under her friend's scrutiny. For their safety, she had to be strong.

"No, I'm not. Really, I'm feeling like shit."

Before she could say anything, Suzie appeared next to Erin. "Antonia, Tex has been calling you. He said to get your butt inside and pick up your phone."

"What the fuck?"

"What the hell?"

She and Erin spoke at the same time.

Suzie shrugged. "I don't know. He just rang my cell and told me I needed to tell you both to get inside."

Antonia looked around to see if there was some sore of surveillance van lurking in the shadows of the street.

How else would Tex know they were both standing outside? It didn't matter anyway, she was still going to stick with her sick story. Tex getting involved only reinforced her decision.

"I'm not feeling well, Suzie, and I don't want to pass whatever it is I've got onto the kids." She took two steps backward and froze when her phone rang again.

"I don't know what's going on." Suzie started. "But I'd answer the phone, I'm betting it's Tex."

Or it could be a murderer. How the heck did he get my number? I want Robot.

What the hell?

Why was Robot her immediate go to thought when she was in danger now? She'd managed to solve her own problems over the years without help. Okay, so this time was different, but she had the police to go to if she needed help.

Erin and Suzie looked at her expectantly as her phone continued to ring. Not answering it would only raise suspicion.

"Hello?"

"Antonia, it's Tex."

She turned her back on the girls and took two steps away from them. "Now's not a really good time Tex, and if it's you that's been calling me I'd really like you to stop."

"Not happening, Antonia. You're Robot's woman and like Erin, Suzie and Brielle, I watch over the women of my SEALs. Now you need to get inside. You'll be safe there." He didn't raise his voice as he spoke, just laid everything out as if he were standing right next to her.

"How do you know I'll be safe here? Being with Erin

and the others is putting them in danger." She hissed down the line. "It's safer if I leave them."

"Antonia, do you trust me?"

What type of question was that? She may not have ever met the guy, but Tex was like some kind of guardian angel.

A hand curled around her waist and she jumped at the contact. "Sheesh, Toni, it's me." Erin's familiar voice washed over her.

"Sorry," she mumbled.

"I don't know what's going on, but if Tex tells you do to something, then you need to do it. You know he's helped find us when we were taken. Trust the guy."

How had her best friend known those were the exact words he'd spoken to her?

"Yes," she whispered into the phone, before clearing her voice. "Yes, I trust you, Tex."

"Good girl. Now get inside. I know you got a call a few minutes ago and I'm trying to trace the origins of it."

How the hell did he know that?

And what was it about the call that sent alarm bells his way.

She didn't want to have this conversation with Erin standing behind her. Although, the second she got inside she'd have to answer questions, not only about her and Robot's marriage, but now about Tex's call and what it was all about.

Geez, her life was heading down shit creek at a rapid pace.

"Erin, go inside, I'll be right in, I promise." She looked

her friend dead in the eye so Erin could see she was going to keep her word.

"Fine, but don't be long."

The second Erin went inside, Antonia turned her focus back to Tex. "What do you know about the call I got? Why haven't other calls I've received have caused you to phone me right away?"

"Why are you still outside?"

"How do you know I'm still outside?" she countered.

A breath huffed down the line. "Look, what I'm about to tell you remains between me and you, you can't tell Erin anything. Will you do that?"

"I don't know, she's my best friend, we share everything with each other." Well, not everything, she thought.

"Have you really told her everything? Tex asked.

Was the guy a mind reader, as well?

"Fine, you've got me. So yes, I'll keep whatever you're about to tell me quiet."

"Good. When Erin and Italy moved into this house, he asked me to set up a discrete security system in and around the house. He wanted to keep her and Kieran safe when he goes away. I also did the same for Joker at his house—Suzie knows about it though."

Okay, so he didn't have super powers, it still didn't explain how he knew about the call.

"Right, well that's good. I'm glad Carlos is keeping his family safe. It still doesn't explain how you knew about my call."

"As I said before, you're Robot's woman, which means I keep an eye on you while he's away, especially after what happened at your complex. He's requested me to look into that situation as well."

It all should sound creepy and in a way it was. A man she'd never met was watching their every move. She wasn't going to have him following her or tracing her calls. She liked her privacy.

"Seeing as Robot asked you to put me under surveillance without discussing it with me, I'm asking you to stop doing whatever it is he asked you do to."

"Not happening. And I know you're probably thinking it's creepy but, rest assured, I don't watch your every move. I only do it when the guys go away and even then, it's not all the time. I do have other things to do. I'm there whenever they need my help, like tracking down guys who arrange for car accidents and then kidnap the occupants of the car."

Ouch.

If Erin had heard Tex's admonishment she'd be asking if Antonia wanted some aloe vera, because she just got burned.

"Right. You're right. I'm sorry."

"Look." Tex's voice softened. "I get you're going through a whole gamut of emotions, what with witnessing a murder. Please understand I'm looking out of you. I'm going to keep you safe and I will find out the origins of that call. But I need you to stay where you are. I can keep you safe at Erin's place, not at some hotel or other place you were probably thinking of escaping to. Trust that I've got this, Antonia."

She sighed and rubbed the bridge of her nose. All she wanted was to have Robot's arms around her. The thought should've freaked her out, but it didn't. She'd been kidding herself to think she wasn't falling for him. Why deny what was becoming more and more obvious with each passing hour? He made her feel safe. And had from the moment she first met him in Vegas.

"Okay. I'll stay here."

"Good, now tell me about the call."

There was no censure in his tone, and for that she was grateful. "I don't know who it was, but I think it had to do with the murder I witnessed. All they said was to keep my mouth shut or I'll pay."

"Damn, I suspected it wasn't a friendly call. I'm betting a burner phone was used to make that call. Leave it with me and when I know something, I'll call you back. Don't ignore me and save my number."

"Will do."

"Good, now get inside. Remember not only am I keeping you safe, I'm keeping your guys safe as well."

Antonia had no idea what he meant by that, but she was learning not to question the man called Tex. "Thanks, Tex. I'll talk to you later."

She disconnected the call and took a deep breath, centering herself before walking into Erin's house.

CHAPTER 9

ANTONIA JERKED AWAKE, her heart pounding against her ribs. She blinked a few times and slowly the furniture in her room began to take shape. It should've been reassuring, except there was something that didn't belong. A figure sat on the edge of her bed.

"It's me, T." The softly spoken words floated over her before she had the chance to open her mouth and scream.

"Robot? You're back."

He chuckled. "Yep, in the flesh."

Antonia didn't think, she just threw the covers back and launched herself at him. Sighing when he's arms closed around her and held her tightly against his hard body. She was immensely glad she'd given him a key after the whole witnessing a murder episode.

She inhaled deeply, and his fresh pine scent filled her senses, calming her jangled nerves.

It had been two weeks since the team had left for their mission. Two long miserable and stressful weeks. Whenever the guys had gone away before, she worried about them, sure. But this trip was different. Before she hadn't believed she had the right to worry about Robot. Now, it was even worse. It was as if a switch had been turned on inside her ever since she found out they were still legally married. She'd spent the whole two weeks worried about him.

Where was he?

Was he okay?

How much danger was he in?

During the weeks he was away, whenever her phone rang, she had another reason to jump at the sound of it. It could've been the creep that had called her the first day Robot had left. Or it could've been someone from the base informing her he'd been hurt or worse killed. Although the only way she'd probably hear about him being hurt was through someone else. As far as she knew listed next-of-kin were the ones notified immediately. And she wasn't that.

But, thankfully, the only calls she received were from the girls or work related.

After the first night at Erin's Tex had assured her if she wanted to return to her apartment she could because he could access the security system and monitor the comings and goings. So, she decided to go back to her place, and slowly everything was returning back to normal.

The murderer still remained at large, but the police had informed her they were getting closer to finding the culprit.

Work had been crazy busy which she was grateful for. She'd been helping the new girl, Lonie, who started the day after Robot had left on his mission, settle into her position as assistant to the marketing director. She'd almost convinced herself the call had been a wrong number and the person was trying to threaten someone else. Until she'd gotten home that night and found a note in her mail box. A note that wasn't postmarked. A note stating they'd found her and she needed to watch out.

She'd picked up her phone to call Tex, but her hands were shaking so badly and her heart pounded loudly in her ears. She decided to take a few minutes to calm herself. It was after eight when she'd gotten home, so she'd gone to her room, turning on every light as she went. After changing into her pajamas she'd climbed into bed, phone on her side table. She'd lain back against her pillows, closed her eyes to center herself and the last thing she'd expected to do was fall asleep, but she had.

And now her man had returned.

"I'm so glad you're back," she whispered into Robot's neck, clinging to him and never wanting to let him go.

Robot tightened his already tight hold on her and she loved every second of being so close to him. "Me too."

She needed his kiss. Needed the reassurance that, even though he felt real in her arms, she wasn't imagining it.

As if he had the same idea, his lips found hers and she sighed into his embrace. They fell back on the bed. Her hands bunched up his t-shirt and slipped beneath the cotton so she could touch the warm had planes of his stomach.

It wasn't enough, she needed more. She wanted it all with him. She wanted to feel the power of his strength as he entered her. Experience the total abandon she's only ever felt when he'd been inside her. Beside her. Over her.

She wrenched her mouth away from his. "I can't do this anymore, Robot."

His body went still then he went to move away, but she pressed her fingers into his back to keep him close.

"Can't what, Antonia. You can't do what anymore?"

In the darkened room his face looked more handsome than she ever thought possible. But there was hint of uncertainty in his features, like he didn't know what she was going to say next. She framed his face with her hands. "Deny my feelings for you. I need you. I want you, Brendan. I want it all."

His eyes widened at her words and she worried she'd been too hasty in blurting out her feelings. Then his lips stretched into a beautiful smile and her heart melted. "All, as in you, me and no clothes?"

She laughed at his explanation. "Yes." To prove her point she reached down and pulled her nightgown over her head.

A few moments later Robot's shirt and jeans joined her nightgown then they were back in each other's arms. Lips devouring as their hands roamed over their bodies. Her fingers reacquainted themselves with the ridges and valleys of his body. Her breath caught in her throat when his lips clamped over her nipples. She arched her back to give him more access. Heat swelled through her and coalesced between her thighs.

Why had she spent so much time denying herself this —being held in Robot's arms? Kissing him. Touching him.

Nothing felt better to her in this moment than having this man worship her.

His tongue trailed a wicked path down her body. Her skin tingled in anticipation of where he would taste next. She lifted her hips, hinting as to what she wanted next.

"All in good time," he mumbled against her inner thigh. He was so close to where she wanted him to be. All he had to was move a little to his left and she'd be happy. But the man had other ideas.

He peppered kisses along her the back of her knee, venturing down to her ankle before starting the slow journey up.

Antonia couldn't take much more of this. All he was giving her were simple caresses, yet her whole body was aflame. Ignited in a way only Robot created within her. Her legs twitched beneath his hands and when his lips finally closed over her clit she moaned long and loud.

"Yes, there. Feels so good."

His fingers gripped her waist, holding her in place. The gesture was totally unnecessary as she had no plans to go anywhere. She was right where she wanted to be.

Robot worked his tongue in and out of her. His fingers tweaked her nipples increasing the sensations flowing through her until she couldn't think. When he inserted two fingers along with his tongue, it set her over the edge. Her orgasm ripped through her and she cried out his name as her body bucked against his mouth and fingers.

Her body rippled with shudders of release when he kissed his way up her belly, swirling his tongue around the swollen peaks of her nipples.

"God, you're going to kill me," she groaned as yet

another delicious shiver coursed through her. Even though she just orgasmed, it wasn't enough. She wanted more. "I want more, Robot. All of you. Inside me."

She pushed on his shoulders and he rolled to the side, releasing her. Antonia reached over his body, her breasts brushing against his chest as she opened the top drawer of her side table and grabbed out a strip of condoms. She rested on her haunches and ripped one of the foil squares off, tossing the rest on the table.

"You ready for round two?" she asked.

He growled and grabbed her around the waist, hauling her against his body. "Round two? T, we haven't even finished round one."

She sighed when his lips crashed over hers. Her fingers found his and together the ripped the packet open then she helped him roll the condom on.

He rolled her onto her back and positioned himself between her thighs, the head of his cock nudged the lips of her pussy. She couldn't wait until he plunged hard inside her.

"You are so beautiful, T. I've missed this," he whispered as he entered her. Her eyes closed as she relished in having him back where he belonged—deep inside of her.

Neither of them moved, their soft breaths were the only sound in the room. Antonia trailed her fingers down his spine until she connected with his taut ass and pressed the hard flesh while lifting her hips at the same time.

This time Robot took the hint and began to move. Slow, measured strokes in and out. Their lips and tongues tangled as he increased the pace, until she had to wrench her mouth away so that she could breath.

The nerve endings at the base of her spine prickled as sensations built inside of her. The electricity generated between the two of them filled her body, energizing her. She lifted her hips and met his hard thrusts, grinding against him to increase the pleasure building within her.

Her fingers tightened their hold on his ass and her back arced up as her second climax hit her. Robot pounded into her, prolonging her release then when he joined her, her inner muscles pulsed around him.

Breathless, he collapsed on top of her and she never wanted him to move.

Robot didn't want to move. He had Antonia back in his arms and he never wanted to let her go.

The past two weeks had been hellish and now he fully understood what Italy, T-Rex and Joker experienced when they were away from their women. It made no sense to him. He'd been away from Antonia since she'd blasted back into his life and he hadn't had any issues. His focus had totally been on the mission and had never wasted a second on thinking about his home in Virginia.

What made this trip so different?

Why had he found his mind wandering when it shouldn't have been?

Fortunately, the one time he had drifted off and almost got into trouble, Italy had been by his side and pulled him back. His friend hadn't said a word to him, just smiled knowingly. He hadn't even bothered to tell Robot to *fuck off* because there was no point.

Robot grimaced as his soft flesh slipped out of Antonia. "I'll be right back," he said and kissed the side of her head.

"Okay."

He disposed of the condom and washed his face. As he padded back into the bedroom and saw she'd snuggled down into the blankets. Her eyes were shut and she looked so contented. His heart skipped a beat and his hands curved into fists as he recalled the text message he'd read earlier. Tex had informed him that she'd received a threatening call from a burner phone the day he'd left. He also mentioned there had been a suspicious person hanging around her apartment complex the last couple of days.

Upon his return, his initial plan was to see her first thing in the morning, but after those messages, he decided he was going straight to her place as soon as he was debriefed. He didn't give a fuck what time of night it was.

Robot walked over to the side of the bed, he'd do anything to keep her safe.

Anything.

He'd scanned the area for the car Tex had described—a late model Chevy Impala sedan, black of course—when he'd arrived, but the area was empty. That didn't mean they wouldn't be back. He had no plans on letting Antonia go anywhere without him.

Commander Black had given them all a couple of days off. Italy and Joker were more than happy with that as they'd missed their girls and kids.

He slid into bed and pulled Antonia into his arms,

curling his body around her before closing his eyes. Everything in this moment was right in his world.

The dream came again, the one where Antonia was captured and had a gun held to her head. Only this time he managed to wake himself up before the gun was fired.

Antonia still lay in his arms, sleeping. Safe. No gun to her head. No faceless guys holding her captive.

He scrubbed a hand down his face. In all his time, with everything he'd seen, he'd never had nightmares about people he cared for.

It was time he faced the facts. He cared more for Antonia than than any of his past relationships and those feelings had started the second she sidled up to the roulette table. He'd been down to his last fifty bucks and was prepared to call it a night, then he'd looked up and had seen her standing next to him. Her dark hair was curled around her shoulders. She wore a sexy black strapless dress that hugged all her curves. She smiled at him, it hit him fair and square in the chest and his dick hardened against the zipper of his trousers. When she'd said, in her sultry tones, to put it on thirteen, her favorite number, he didn't give it a second thought and placed his own last chip on the number. Thirteen had come up and his winning streak began so he'd kept her close, which wasn't difficult as she hadn't seemed to want to move away from him.

The idea of marrying her may have been a spur of the moment idea, but he'd been well aware of what he was doing and what he was asking of Antonia. He didn't regret his decision then, and he didn't regret it now.

What did Antonia feel though?

Last night she'd said she wanted it all, but did that mean she only wanted his body, or did she want to make their marriage real?

Was the possible threat hanging over her head the reason she wanted to sleep with him or was it because she finally faced her feelings for him?

Fuck, he needed to stop this merry-go-round of thoughts before he went insane. Sliding away from Antonia, and making sure he didn't wake her, he reached down and grabbed his jeans, pulling them on as he exited the bedroom.

He walked into the kitchen and grabbed a bottle of water from the fridge. Looking out the window, the early morning fingers of dawn were stretching across the courtyard. This was where Antonia was standing when she witnessed the murder. The area was still shadowed so he couldn't see if there was still evidence of the crime.

Warm arms slid around his waist. "Why are you up so early?"

He put the bottle down and stared out the window for a few seconds more. Did she know how having her seek him out made him feel? Probably not, as he was only now coming to the conclusion of how important Antonia was to him. Like her, he'd denied it for so long it had become second nature to him.

He turned and hooked his arms loosely around her waist. "Question is, why are you up so early?"

He lowered his lips to hers and pulled her tight against him. His cock reacted immediately to her closeness. Her nails dug into his back and he welcomed the sting of pain. He needed the closeness they'd shared the previous evening again. Bending his knees, he scooped her up in his arms and strode back to her bedroom.

Once they got over the threshold he slid her down his body, her silky robe bunching between them.

"I could get used to this," Antonia murmured as she reached for his waistband and pulled his zipper down. His hard cock sprung out and he inhaled deeply when her fingers closed over him.

"I could get used to *this*," he responded when she went to her knees, anticipation firing through him waiting for the second her mouth took him in. He groaned when his wish came true.

His fingers entwined in her hair, holding her head in place. Her fingers squeezed the base of his cock as her tongue swirled over his tip. Closing his eyes, he gave himself over to the sensations of her fingers stroking and squeezing him while her tongue laved his engorged flesh. He was lost in the magic her tongue was creating, and willed himself to keep it together so he didn't lose his load in her mouth.

As much as he loved what she was doing to him, he wanted to sink into her body. Reaching down he pulled her away from him. His lips found hers with unerring accuracy and he frog marched them back to her bed. He opened her robe, delighted to see her naked body.

"God, you're so beautiful, T," he said as he leaned down and took a nipple in his mouth.

Everything about them was right. He would do whatever needed to keep her right by his side.

Forever.

THE SUN FILTERED THROUGH HER BLINDS WHEN ANTONIA opened her eyes. Thank God, it was Friday and all she had to do was get through the work day then she'd have the weekend to look forward to. She stretched, her body aching in all the right places, reminding her just what she and Robot got up to during the night. She couldn't believe he had come to see her on his return.

Why had he done that? Not that she was complaining, but why didn't he go home? She would've thought he'd be anxious to sleep in his own bed.

She sat up, holding the sheet against her naked body. The room was empty, the only sign of his presence was the dent in the pillow beside her.

Grabbing up her robe, she tied the sash as she walked out the door. "Robot? Are you here?"

Surely, he wouldn't have left her, not after coming to her place in the middle of the night. The shower wasn't running so he wasn't there. Disappointment flowed through her when she found the kitchen was empty. Had he just come to her in the middle of the night to slake his need? Why had she thought their relationship was changing? Just because she wanted it to happen, didn't mean Robot felt the same way.

She couldn't believe he'd actually upped and left her while she was sleeping. No sooner had she finished the thought, her front door opened and the man in question stepped through, drink carrier in one hand and a brown carrier bag looped over his other hand.

"Where the hell did you go?" She blurted out, the

second he closed the door. Relief flowed through her even though she was annoyed she'd woken up and he hadn't been there.

"Good morning to you too, T. And I would've thought it was obvious—I got us breakfast" The corners of his mouth lifted as if he was amused with her affront.

"You could've at least left a note." She grumbled as she crossed her arms over her chest. Her stomach rumbled as the aroma from the bag he carried reached her.

He placed the drinks and bag on her side table, before walking over to her. He cupped her chin. "I'm sorry I didn't leave a note. I thought I'd be back before you woke up." He dropped a soft kiss on her lips. "Now you need to eat then get ready. You've got to work today."

"Tell me something I don't already know," she grumbled and pulled away from his touch. If she didn't, she'd drag him back to her bedroom and have her wicked way with him.

He chuckled as he collected the items again and headed toward her kitchen. As he walked past, she stayed right where she ewas and admired the fit of his jeans around his ass. The ass she'd finally been able to sink her fingers into.

"What the fuck is this," he demanded and walked back into her line of vision. In his left hand was the note she'd received the previous day.

Oh shit.

What had she been thinking leaving it in the middle of her kitchen table? Well, she hadn't expected a midnight visit from Robot. That's for sure.

She straightened her spine and looked him head on.

No way was she going to back down from him. "I think it's pretty obvious what it is."

The paper crumpled in his hand as he strode toward her. "And when did this lovely piece of mail arrive? I know for damn sure you haven't told Tex about it either. Jesus, Antonia don't you know how fucking serious this is?"

Now her own anger was spiking. He had no right to speak to her like that, regardless of the fact that, in the eyes of the law, they're a married couple. Or that they'd spent the night together. "Of course, I know how serious it is. I'm the one who witnessed a murder. I'm the one who received threatening phone calls and now threatening letters. Not you. So how about you back off with the over protective Navy SEAL shit."

"I will not back off. This is who I am and how I do things." He scrubbed a hand over his face. "I'm going to call Tex.

He stormed out of the room, the slamming of her front door echoed through the apartment.

"Well, that went well." She muttered as pulled one of the cups out of the cupholder. Taking a sip of the brew the warm liquid flowed through her. Robot's reaction shouldn't have surprised her. His unexpected arrival at her apartment had made her forget all about the note for a few hours.

She could just imagine the conversation going on between Robot and Tex right now. Both men would be angry at her for not calling them straightaway. Tex would've blown off her concern at calling too late. She wondered if the man actually slept. Or if he was ever off the clock. From what she knew he worked from home, there was no knocking off at five-thirty and walking out an office building for Tex.

Robot was the same, never totally off the job, always waiting for the phone call to come that could send them away without much notice. Now, she'd given Robot something else to worry about, when he didn't need. Antonia had no idea what the mission he'd just been on had been like. He was probably still decompressing after everything he'd seen and the last thing he expected when he came to her was to find a threatening note.

Why had she left it on the table? Why hadn't she thrown it away. Or burned it even. Out of sight out of mind and Robot would never have known about it.

Sometimes she wondered how different her life would be if Erin and Carlos had never reunited. She never would've seen Robot again and got reacquainted with him.

If she didn't know him, he wouldn't be on the phone now to Tex talking about this situation.

And if you *didn't know him, you'd be facing this all by yourself and you'd be at the mercy of cops who had numerous other cases to deal with.*

A shiver wracked her body and she wrapped her arms around herself at the truth of her inner thoughts. Alternatively, if her life hadn't taken the road it had, she wouldn't have witnessed the murder and wouldn't be in this situation.

She'd still be in New York. And, yeah, there was no guarantee she wouldn't have witnessed some other nasty crime if she'd stayed there.

"Oh my God. Just stop it Antonia." She practically yelled the words to the empty apartment. Her heart beat erratically against her chest and her breaths came in short, sharp bursts. Was she having some sort of panic attack? Life hadn't been kind to her in Virginia. But she was stronger than this. Nope, she wasn't losing her mind.

"Stop what?"

Of course, he'd return when she was going through a small mental breakdown. "Nothing. It's nothing. Everything's great."

He hands closed over her shoulders and she willed herself to stay a stiff as a statue. Why was he being so nice when ten minutes ago he was so angry?

Her eyes drifted shut when he kissed the back of her neck softly. His hands now looped loosely around her waist and he tugged her so her back rest against his chest. "I'm sorry, T."

This Robot, the man who was sweet and gentle, was so hard to resist. Yet she needed to. After last night, hell the past two weeks, she'd been battling with keeping her heart closed off from allowing Robot in. Her family history proved that relationships didn't work out for the Rocca family. She had to remember that.

Yet, she was failing miserably at it. Last night, the way she'd been so happy to see him, had shown her she'd fallen in love with her Vegas husband and that scared the crap out of her.

CHAPTER 10

Robot looked around the group of men seated at his dining room table. "You there, Tex?"

"Yep. Hey guys."

A chorus of 'heys' went around the table.

"Right, let's get started," Robot said before anyone had a chance to ask questions. He wanted this meeting over and done so he could get back to Antonia. After their argument this morning, she'd accepted his apology then got ready for work. He'd followed her there then went back to his place to arrange this meeting.

Antonia was safe at work. Her building had good security and he made her promise she wouldn't leave the office by herself. She rolled her eyes and started to protest until he'd told her about the car Tex had seen lurking around her work place. He hated seeing her face go pale and fear creep into her eyes, but she needed to know exactly how much the situation had escalated.

"Why are we here, Robot, and why is Tex on the

phone?" Italy asked. "Not that we don't like talking you, Tex, but we just got back last night. I wanted to spend time with Erin and Kieran—"

"I know," Robot jumped in. "And I wouldn't have called you guys here if it wasn't important. Antonia's in danger."

Immediately, the five men at the table sat up straight and leaned forward. "What the hell, Robot? What's going on?" This was from Italy. His concern was understandable seeing as, out of all of them, he'd known Antonia the longest.

"I'll let Tex explain. Go ahead, Tex."

"Right, thanks Robot. Here's what we know so far. The person who killed the woman at Antonia's complex is still at large and the police don't have anything concrete to go on, other than identifying the woman and speaking to her family. Even Antonia's statement and brief description haven't helped. It's like this guy's disappeared."

"But I'm guessing he hasn't?" asked T-Rex.

"No. The day you guys left, Antonia received a phone call. All I know is the guy said for her to watch out. Did she mention anything more to you about it, Robot?"

"Negative, all she said was that she'd received threatening calls. But we were arguing at the time so any chance of her giving me any information about it freely was slim."

"Fuck, Robot, is arguing all you and Antonia do?" This came from Red. "You guys have a weird ass type of relationship."

The last thing Robot wanted to do was get into the ins and outs of his and Antonia's relationship. Admittedly, they had a lot to work out, but he wasn't going to walk away from her.

Not now.

Not ever.

"We're not here to discuss our relationship. Go on, Tex."

"Right, she received a call. I traced it back to a burner phone, but then the lead went cold, which pisses me off, because usually I can find anything. My thinking is, this has to be gang related. That said, the deceased woman's family believe she wasn't involved with anyone from a gang."

"We all know how threatening these guys can be. She was probably scared shitless to say anything to anyone in her family," Cowboy commented.

"More than likely. Or her family knows and are scared they're going to come after them so they're keeping their mouths shut." The sound of Tex clicking away on a keyboard sounded over the line, before continuing. "I've had Antonia's place under surveillance and the past four days a car has been lurking around the place during the day. Parks in different places each time."

"When she's not there?" Joker asked. "That makes no sense."

"You're right, Joker. From what I've been able to observe they leave about an hour after Antonia arrives home. I agree their actions don't make any sense. The bastards are smart though. They park in different places and in a way that makes getting eyes on the plates impossible. I've tried every possible camera angle, zoomed in as far as possible and still nothing. Initially, I thought it was a person visiting someone in the complex, but no one gets out of the car and it's parked there for over eight hours."

Robot sat back and mulled over what Tex said. When they'd left this morning, he hadn't noticed the car and he'd looked at every vehicle they passed. "Is it there now, Tex?"

"Let me check. While I do that, why don't you tell them about the letter."

Robot reached into his back pocket and pulled out the piece of paper. He unfolded it and placed it in the middle of the table. "She read it yesterday and said it wasn't post-marked so it had to be hand delivered."

The guys looked at the letter, fists clenching and lips thinning in anger even more as they each read the words for themselves. "This is bullshit, Robot. We can't let anything happen to Antonia again." This came from T-Rex. A few months ago, T-Rex and Brielle had been captured from her apartment building, so Robot could understand the underlying venom in T-Rex's tone.

"That's why we're all here—to make sure nothing happens to her."

"The car's not there, Robot." Tex's tinny voice boomed around the room.

Robot pushed away from the table and stood. Immediately his lower back began to itch. A signal when shit was about to hit the fan during a mission. "What the fuck? This is making no fucking sense at all. A car sits outside her place all day. No one gets in and out, yet a note is put in Antonia's mailbox at her apartment. Now you're saying the car's not there? Something's not right."

"Robot?"

The seriousness of Tex's tone didn't abate his intuition, it magnified it a hundred percent. "Yeah, Tex?"

"The car's outside her work."

Robot's heart lurched to his stomach. "Fuck, I should've stayed with her. Kept a watch on her. What was I thinking?"

A hand landed on his shoulder and he looked up to see that Italy was beside him. His friend's gaze intense but resolved. "She's going to be fine. Can you get eyes on her in the building Tex?"

Adrenaline pumped through Robot's veins, he wanted to rush out the door, jump in his car and go to Antonia. The need to see her and know she was safe threatened to overwhelm his normally cool head. He'd never felt this way before and now he fully understood everything Italy and Joker had gone through when their women had been taken.

He loved her.

He fucking loved Antonia and wanted nothing more than to be able to tell her that. He should've said it earlier. This morning when he kissed her goodbye. God, he hoped he had the chance to tell her.

"Robot?"

Tex's voice pulled him from his inner thoughts. "Yeah?"

"I can only see into the reception area of her workplace. Everything looks fine. I can also see action happening on her computer. I'm confident she's safe."

"For now," he muttered, before looking up at the guys. "T-Rex, is Brielle at work or working from home today?"

"She's home. And I should mention she's quit her job. She'll be finishing up in a couple of weeks."

Robot sensed there was more to that story, but he'd

ask T-Rex about it later. "Right, good. Italy and Joker, you need to get in contact with Erin and Suzie. Get them to go to Brielle's place. The security there is tight and Tex can keep an eye on them."

"He could do the same at my place you know," grumbled Italy.

"Yes, I know, but these assholes know Antonia has been there. At least at Brielle's place we will know for certain that they're safe," Robot insisted.

"Fuck, you're right." Italy dug into his pocket, pulled out his phone and strode down the hallway.

Robot noticed both T-Rex and Joker were doing the same. Cowboy and Red, now the only single guys on the team, still sat at the table.

"Shit." Tex's voice boomed in the room.

Immediately the itching at the small of Robot's back increased. "What? What's wrong, Tex."

"Fire alarm is going off in Antonia's building. They're evacuating."

"Fuck." Robot clenched his hands into fists. "Can you keep eyes on her, Tex."

"Yes, I'm pulling up all the traffic cameras in the area. But you guys need to haul ass. I don't like this."

"Fuck, this is not good. Not good at all," Robot muttered as he thrust back his chair.

He looked at his five teammates back in the room with him. All of them had their game faces on. One of their own was in danger and they were ready for action. "It's go-time."

"WHY DO THESE SIRENS HAVE TO BE SO OBNOXIOUS?"

"To make sure we don't ignore it." Antonia said, laughing as she walked with, Lonie, the new girl who'd she'd been training.

As they walked, she noticed Lonie had her handbag with her. "Oh, Lonie, company evacuation policy is you have to leave all personal belongings behind, can't even take a cell phone because of the threat of remote detonation if this is a bomb scare. Why don't you leave it on this table, and we'll pick it up once we're allowed back into the building?"

In a flash the woman's hand shot out and grasped Antonia tight around her upper arm. "Hey, what are you doing?" Antonia tried to break free but, Lonie tightened her grip.

Her normally pleasant features turned sinister and her lip curled in disgust. "Listen to me, bitch, you act normal and don't bring any attention to us. If you do, I'll kill you."

Antonia's adrenaline spiked and she wished she'd thought to grab her cellphone, even though it was against the rules. "Who are you?" she asked figuring if she got out of this alive, having as much information as possible would be a good thing. "Is your name even Lonie?"

"Who I am or what my name is doesn't matter. What matters is that we get out of here and I deliver you to the guy who paid me. Once that's done, I'm gone and you never have to see me again."

"Hey Antonia, everything okay here?" She looked up and found her boss Evan striding over. Lonie released her tight grip a fraction, but not enough for Antonia to break free.

She glanced at Lonie, her sinister expression gone and she'd transformed back to the friendly woman Antonia known the last two weeks. God, she couldn't believe she'd fallen right into the woman's trap when she was clearly unhinged. The question was, did Antonia try to indicate to Evan she was in trouble or did she believe that Lonie would kill her?

Lonie squeezed her arm and that gave her the answer she needed. She couldn't potentially put Evan at risk too. "Sorry Evan, this alarm is giving me a headache. But we're fine, Lonie is a little anxious in crowds so I told her to hang on to me. We'll see you out the front."

"Okay, if you're sure." Of all the times for Evan to be observant he had to pick today.

"Yep, we're sure. Thanks Evan. You probably need to get out there quickly, seeing as you're the boss and all." She attempted to laugh but it sounded more like a shrill than a genuine chuckle.

She breathed out when he finally upped his pace and strode ahead of them.

"Good," Lonie murmured as she reached into her bag. "Put these on."

Antonia looked at the items in her hand. "You have got to be kidding me? I thought you didn't want to draw attention. If I put on those glasses and ballcap I'm going to stand out like a sore thumb."

Antonia was going to fight with everything she had. She needed to let Lonie believe she was going to go along with everything she wanted. Antonia had no doubt that Tex was aware of the situation going on in her building. The guy was probably looking at ways to hack into all the security cameras around the area. She needed to give him a message, let him know which direction she was being taken.

Glancing up she spied the security camera over the side door they were exiting through. If she could somehow look up and say something maybe it will help Tex. Fortunately there was a crowd of people slowing them down so she had a little time.

Keeping her head up and eyes straightforward, aimed directly at the camera, asking the question she'd already asked before. She had to give Tex as much information as possible. "You're working for the guy who killed the woman in my apartment complex, aren't you?" She'd pitched her voice low but had made sure she pronounced each word slowly and clearly.

"I told you before, it doesn't matter who I work for. I've got a job to do and I'm doing it. Now put these on the second we get through the door." Lonie shoved the items into her side again.

Antonia snatched them. "You won't get away with this. You will be found, and I wouldn't like to be you when you are."

"Honey, I wouldn't worry about me. I'd worry about what's going to happen to you when I hand you off." Lonie's words held a wealth of menace and Antonia strived to keep up the bravado she'd clung to the last few minutes.

As they passed under the camera she looked up and mouthed *help me, Tex* and prayed the man got the message.

The second they stepped outside, Antonia put on the

glasses and the plain black hat. She supposed the good thing about wearing the items was she'd be recognizable in the cameras and Tex could track her movements.

Lonie pulled them in the opposite direction than everyone else was going. Sirens wailed in the air as police and fire trucks descended on the scene.

They veered down the side street next to her building. Antonia darted her gaze around, looking in every direction for a way to escape and not getting herself killed in the process. She was also hoping to see a team of guys dressed in black to jump out of the shadows and rescue her. She longed to see Robot's familiar silhouette bearing down on them, ready to pluck her to safety.

They stopped beside a black Dodge Challenger. The back passenger door opened. Before she had time to think, Lonie pushed her forward and a tanned hand grabbed her just above her wrist and yanked her into the car.

Antonia yelped at the violence of the movement. She was rewarded with a slap across her cheek. A sting of pain shot through her and she bit her lip to hold back her cry. She was shoved across the seat.

"I delivered the bitch as requested. Where's my money?" Lonie spat the words at the man sitting next to Antonia.

The guy pulled out a gun and shot Lonie straight between her eyes.

Antonia screamed as the woman hit the pavement with a dull thud.

"Fucking drive." The shooter shouted, and the car shot off with a squeal of rubber.

How the hell was she going to survive this? The guy sitting next to her just committed cold-blooded murder and appeared not to give a shit about it.

"Who are you? What do you want with me?"

"I would've thought it was obvious what I want to do with you, Antonia Rocca, but if it needs explaining here it is. I'm going to make sure you're no longer a factor in the murder of that bitch Ricki. The cops haven't come close to finding me. To make sure it stays that way, I'm cleaning up all the loose ends before I move on to my next project."

Every word that came out of the man's mouth was without emotion and very eloquent. At odds with the plethora of tattoos covering each of his arms and climbing up his neck from the collar of the shirt he wore. His long hair fell across his face in a familiar way. He looked like a guy who belonged to the roughest gangs in the city, and probably did. But he sounded like a man who would be comfortable sitting a board table surrounded by some of the richest men in the country. It just proved how wrong it was to judge a book by its cover. You never know what lay between the pages.

"You're the guy I saw that day?" *Fuck* why did she go and say that? Why didn't she say she had no idea what he was talking about? Not that he'd believe her, he didn't look like a man who made mistakes when it came to important things like eliminating witnesses to a murder.

"An unfortunate outcome and now I must deal with you."

Her heart dropped to her stomach and she wished Robot had taken it upon himself to act as her personal bodyguard and stayed with her all day. "What are you going to do with me?"

How the hell could she sound so calm? Her insides were shaking like jello just out of its mold.

He leaned forward and smiled, his teeth stained yellow with nicotine. "Where would be the fun if I told you that."

In a blur of movement his arm rose and fired across her cheek. Her ears buzzed and black spots dotted her vision as pain racked her whole face.

"Now I think it's time you slept." A cloth covered her nose and mouth and the pungent aroma of chemicals surrounded her. She fought against his hold, but it was hopeless. Her head was still swimming from his blows and she sank into the blackness.

CHAPTER 11

Robot paced out front of Antonia's office building. The threat to the occupants had been proven to be unfounded and everyone was slowly returning to their work places. Everyone except Antonia. He and his teammates had combed through the mass of people, but hadn't been able to locate her.

It didn't help that he wasn't familiar with the people she worked with.

"I didn't find her," Italy said as he walked up, the rest of the guys in the team following. From the looks on their faces, Robot knew they had the same news.

"Have you heard from Tex?" asked Joker.

"Not, since just before we arrived. He said once he had something, he'd call us back."

"Why's it taking him so long? We've been here over forty minutes," commented Red.

And Robot's anxiety levels had risen with every passing minute. His instincts were screaming at him that

Antonia had been taken and the fire alarm was just a diversion.

Four cops sprinted past them, quickly followed by two paramedics.

"What the fuck?" he said and started to follow them. Whatever they were going to wasn't good.

He didn't need to look to see if his men followed him. He knew they would. He raced along the sidewalk and down the side street, screeching to a halt when he spied a pair of legs on the ground. A pair of feminine legs wearing shoes he'd seen in Antonia's closet.

His knees buckled when he spied the line of red coming from the body. A silent *No* echoed in his mind. It couldn't be her. He couldn't lose her. Not now. Not when he'd decided he was going to do anything to keep her at his side.

An arm banded around him and hauled him upright.

"It's not her," Italy said in his ear. "It's not Antonia."

The words finally penetrated the black haze that consumed him, and he turned to his team mate. "How do you know?"

"Because this is a blonde and Antonia is a brunette."

He made a move to get closer, to reassure himself what Italy said was correct. He needed to know without a doubt the woman lying dead on the ground wasn't Antonia.

"I'm sorry, sir, but I can't let you get any closer." One of the policemen who'd raced through the building held up a hand stopping him from proceeding any further.

"Please, you need to let me just check to make sure the

victim isn't my wife. She works in the building you were just in. I can't find her."

Logically, his mind was telling him it wasn't her, but his heart wouldn't let go of the *what if it was her*. Some of his desperation must have shown through, because the officer gave a quick nod and stepped to the side.

Having been given the all clear he should've been rushing past the man, yet his feet wouldn't move. The directions from his brain to his feet seemed to have been lost.

"Sir, you can go check the victim." The officer repeated.

He got about three feet away when he stopped. The women's eyes stared unseeingly up at the sky. Why hadn't someone closed them? Her facial features were as different to Antonia's as sun and rain.

Relief slammed through him with the force of recoil from a dessert eagle gun. The officer stepped up next to him. "Is this your wife, sir?"

"No," he whispered then cleared his throat. "No, it's not."

He nodded. "Do you know who she is?"

"Sorry, I can't help you." Now that he had confirmation, Robot needed to get back to the task of trying to find her. And to phone Tex. It had been too long without any communication from the computer wizard. "I hope you get to the bottom of who the victim is." He nodded to the police officer then walked back to his team.

"It wasn't her, was it?" asked Italy.

"No, you were right," he sighed. "I don't know who it is. What the fuck is going on here? A false alarm with her building and now a murder just around the corner from it. I don't like this shit."

"We *all* don't like it," said Cowboy. "My wrist is itching like an ornery bull waiting to fly out of the chute at a rodeo."

Robot shook his head at Cowboy's analogy. The guy had been an upcoming rodeo star until he gave it all away and joined the Navy. He never did explain why he'd changed careers and the guys never asked. They all had their own reasons for doing what they did with their lives. Just like he hadn't elaborated on why he and Antonia got married.

His phone rang, and he pulled it out of his pocket, glancing at the screen. "It's Tex." The guys all crowded around and hit accept and then the speaker button. "Tex, Antonia's missing."

"I know, put me on speaker so I can speak to everyone."

"You're already on speaker. What can you tell us? Why has it taken so long for you to get back to us?"

"I know, for some reason there was an issue with the cameras in the area around her building. It happened just after I told you about the alarm."

"Fuck." Robot didn't like the sound of that. He'd been counting on Tex having access to the cameras to be able to pinpoint what happened to Antonia. "Do you have any footage at all that can help us. My *wife* is missing."

"I haven't lost anyone yet, and I'm not going to start now."

Running a hand over his head, Robot took a couple of deep breaths to quell his anger. "Sorry, I know. I know. I think I need to step back." He looked over at Italy. He'd always considered the man his closest friend and the perfect second-in-command, as well as had the rest of the team. Italy nodded in answer to his silent message. "Italy's going to take the lead."

"Right, here's the status," Tex continued. "Whoever tried to take down the system didn't do a very good job at it. It took me awhile, but I was able to piece together footage from the foyer of her company office, to the building foyer, to the cameras around the building."

Robot bit back the orders he wanted to bark out, but he knew Italy would ask the questions he would.

"Do you have an idea where Antonia is or not?" Italy questioned.

"Robot, your girl is a smart one. She looked at the cameras and gave me silent messages."

"What did she say? Did she give you any idea of what was happening to her?" Robot demanded, uncaring that he was supposed to be taking a backseat.

"When she passed a camera she said something to the blonde next to her." Robot's spine tingled and he glanced back down the alley where a blonde woman lay dead.

"Her name is Lonie and Antonia asked if she worked for the guy who's killing she witnessed."

"And what did she say?" This came from Italy.

"Because she wasn't enunciating her words as deliberately as Antonia, I only caught a few, but she something along the lines of it didn't matter who she worked for and then she handed Antonia what looked like a hat and glasses."

"Making her unrecognizable," murmured Joker.

"Yep, that's what I think. She gave me one final message when she passed the camera over the fire exit door—she said, *help me Tex*."

"Fuck. She's amazing." Robot murmured. Even amidst the danger of the situation she'd found herself in, she had the wherewithal to leave messages she knew Tex would be able to find.

"Tex, we're still at Antonia's building. The woman she left with is lying on the pavement, shot through the eyes," T-Rex commented.

"Fuck, really?" he said incredulously. Somehow Robot suspected Tex wasn't easily surprised.

"Yeah, not sure that's the type of payment she was expecting," muttered Robot.

The sound of fingers flying over keyboard sounded over the phone. Robot had no idea what the man was doing, but hopefully he was finding out where Antonia was. Or at least where she was headed. The longer they stood twiddling their thumbs, the further Antonia got away from them.

"Okay I've managed to get some footage of the area where you are." Tex said just when Robot was getting impatient for some information.

Robot made a move to lean closer to the phone, but Italy stilled his movement. He sent Robot a *Trust me, I've got this* look.

Fuck, he was supposed to be taking a back seat, but he couldn't seem to stop himself from taking over. He took a step back and Italy nodded. "Tex, what have you go for us?" he asked.

"When Antonia left the building she donned a black

ball cap and sunglasses. The woman with her didn't do anything to disguise herself. They disappeared around the corner."

Robot clenched his fists, they knew she disappeared around the corner, they were standing by the dead body, why didn't Tex get that?

"Fuck." Tex exclaimed.

"What?" asked Italy.

"There was no fight, whoever was in the car just shot the blonde, closed the door and drove away with Antonia."

"Which direction, Tex and what sort of car?" Italy bounced on his feet and Robot recognized the sign he was anxious to get out on the road.

"I'm about to send the coordinates to you. I'm able to track them. They Impala is still out the front of the building. I'll let the cops know about it. But they're now in a stolen Dodge Challenger. I'm guessing they didn't realize the owner of the car has it registered with one of those organizations that tracks cars. We'll be able to get these fuckers."

"Thank fuck," breathed out Robot.

They needed to get moving.

"Let's go, Team," he said.

Hang on, T. Hang on. I'm coming. He mentally sent her the message as he strode to the car.

THROUGH THE FOG OF THE DRUGS USED TO KNOW HER OUT, a sense of calm had settled over Antonia. Why wasn't she panicking? She was being kidnapped and taken to God knew where. She should be scared out of her mind, but she wasn't. Deep in her heart she had no doubt Robot Tex, and the guys were working on a way to rescue her, like they'd done before. Believing that help was on the way was the only thing keeping her sane at the moment.

What she had to do was make sure she didn't get on the bad side of the guy whose meaty thigh rested against hers.

Concentrating on her breathing, making sure it remained even so he wasn't aware she'd woken up, she opened her eyes a little to see if she could make out where they were.

Damn, she'd have to move her head to get a good look.

"How much further?" The guy next to her spoke.

"Not long, maybe another ten minutes." She assumed it was the driver speaking.

"And everything is in place?"

"Yeah, Lars, is ready and waiting for us."

Who the fuck was Lars? And what was waiting for them when they arrived?

The car jolted as it hit a pot hole and, even though everything in her screamed to stay away from the guy next to her, she allowed her body to fall against him.

He shoved her back, hard, and her cheek slammed against the door. Pain burst through her already bruised face and it was impossible to hold back the grunt of pain.

"Ahh sleeping beauty is awake. Perfect. We're almost at our destination."

Antonia gave up all pretense of being asleep, turned and glared at him. "What are you going to do with me?"

He lifted a shoulder but didn't answer. The guy was cooler than an ice block. His brown eyes were completely void of emotion. The man certainly had no soul, no one who possessed one would be able to murder two women without flinching like he did.

God, she hoped Robot was on somehow on his way to her, she definitely didn't want to be his third victim. Actually, she probably wouldn't be his third victim, he more than likely had a slew of victims he'd taken out.

"Who are you? And why do you want me?" she persisted.

"Who I am is of no concern to you. As for what I want with you. Well," he looked her over and a shiver of revulsion crept over her skin like a snake slithering over a rock. "I haven't quite decided."

The guy was lying, his mind was full of what he wanted to do with her, and Antonia guessed it wasn't to have lunch.

The words were on the tip of her tongue. She wanted to blurt out that he wouldn't get away with what he had planned, and she would be rescued, but how could she be so sure? Her cellphone was in her purse which was probably still sitting in her desk drawer. While Tex's reputation was second to none, there was still the chance he hadn't been able to see which car she'd been bundled into.

Stop it. Her mind yelled at her. She had to believe she would be rescued. That, by some miracle, in a few hours she'd be wrapped in Robot's arms.

She closed her eyes on the thought of never being able to see him again. Touch him. Kiss him. *Love* him.

Like she had decided the night before in his arms,

denying she loved and wanted him was useless. She could no longer deny that she'd loved him since that first night in Vegas. She absolutely fell head over heels in love with him at first sight. Maybe it had taken her a little while to get on board with it, but now she was a full-fledged member of the love train and she had no desire to get off. If she did, it would be with Robot beside her, holding her hand, guarding and protecting her like only he could.

She had to hang on. Had to believe deep in her bones he was only a few minutes behind her. He'd rescued her before and not just when she'd been taken with Erin. Her wandering soul was found the moment their eyes met across a roulette table.

The car stopped, and she sat a little straighter. Looking out the window, she didn't recognize her surroundings. They were in some residential area where the houses looked like they could use a good coat of paint. The porch of the house they were parked in front of had an array of lawn chairs situated on it, the broken down fence surrounding it would easily be taken away on a strong wind. The yard was more weed than grass and the only thing that looked reasonably healthy was an old tree that stood large and proud in the far left corner.

Antonia didn't have time to study anything else before the door was opened and she was pulled out of the car.

"Don't even thinking about screaming, bitch, because no one will come running. Not here." Her kidnapper spoke in her ear as he pulled up the pathway to the front of the house.

Of course, she wasn't going to scream, she wasn't

stupid. And she was well aware the chance of anyone coming to her rescue was zero.

The door opened the second their feet hit the porch.

"I've got everything set up." A raspy voice stated.

Antonia looked up and saw a man with stringy, shoulder length hair that could do with a good cut and wash. This must be Lars, the guy they'd been talking about in the car. Like the man holding her captive, his eyes held a sinister glare touched with a twisted excitement.

Fuck, did they all get turned on by torturing women?

"Excellent." She was jolted to a halt before they crossed the threshold. The hand around her arm squeezed a little tighter and she looked at the man holding her. If she thought his eyes were dead before, now they blazed with life, as if the thought of torturing her, or whatever they planned, pleased him. "If you cooperate with everything I say, you may just get out of here alive. Maybe." He then leaned over and kissed her on the lips, she fought back the urge to vomit all over him. Perhaps she shouldn't and see how he dealt with being covered in throw up.

He shoved her through the door and she stumbled, reaching to grab at anything to prevent herself from falling flat on her face. Her fingers clashed with Lars's sweaty ones.

The second she was upright she snatched her hand away. "Keep your hands off me, asshole."

Her reward for her sass was another slap across her cheek by Lars, the one that hadn't already received two slaps. At least she'd have matching bruises.

"Lars, don't touch until I say so." The words held a

wealth of authority. It looked like Mr. Kidnapper was the only one allowed to hand out physical punishment. "Take her to the room."

Lars grabbed her and marched her through the house. What little glimpses she caught the rooms she walked past, the house was a mess and it smelled funky too—a combination of old shoes, sweat and garbage. She couldn't believe people actually lived here. Maybe they didn't, maybe it was kept for this reason only, as a place to bring people to torture or rape before they killed them.

Antonia shuddered in fear, sweat beaded her brow and her stomach heaved. She swallowed down the bile, her throat burning. She hated letting the word rape even factor into what might happen to her, but she had to be realistic, there was a good chance she could be sexually assaulted.

"Wait here. Boss will be back soon." At least she had a name she could refer to her kidnapper as, seeing he hadn't introduced himself to her.

The door shut behind Lars, and Antonia looked around. The room was as dirty as the rest of the house. In one corner sat a single bed, the comforter had seen better days and she couldn't tell what color it was, or had been. The window was boarded up so there was no escape there. Swiveling, her gaze landed on a long white table with a number of items laid across the top. Clutching her stomach, she walked over to it, but a closer inspection didn't make her any feel better. Knives of all different shapes and sizes and things that looked like big pliers were laid out before her.

"I see you're familiarizing yourself with a few of my favorite items." Boss walked back in.

What would happen if she grabbed a knife and threw it at him? She'd never thrown a knife in her life, but desperate times called for desperate matters. Her hand inched out, but, before she could even get close to picking up one of the shiny metal items, Boss's arms closed around her waist, lifting her off her feet. In a quick motion Robot would've been proud of, he tossed her on the bed. She landed with a thump and a spring from the mattress dug into her lower back.

"That was a big mistake."

She'd had enough of playing docile victim. It wasn't in her nature and she wasn't going to start now. No doubt if Robot could see her, he'd tell her to back down and play it cool, but the fear and fight instincts had taken over and flowed through her, more so now after seeing those metal items on the table.

"No, the mistake you made was taking me. You're going to regret it. It won't be me who'll end up dead by the end of the day, it will be *you*." She reached down, took off her shoe and flung it at him, hitting him square in the chest.

Antonia was well aware she was poking the bear, but if it kept her from getting up close and personal with any of those instruments of death on the table then she'd do it. She went to grab her other shoe, but Boss moved swiftly and had her arms above her head before she could take a breath.

"You just keep making mistakes don't you, bitch? I had

planned to play nice with you, now that's never going to happen."

A searing, burning sensation slammed into the top of her right thigh and she screamed. She looked down and saw the hilt of a knife sticking out of her leg. Her breaths came in short, sharp bursts as the pain rippled through her.

"If I'd gone a little further to the left, I'd have hit the femoral artery. That would mean you'd bleed out and I don't want that. I'm quite adept with my knife skills." Boss leaned in close and swiped his tongue down her cheek. "I'm going to have fun."

Agonizing pain from the knife still in her leg kept her pinned to the bed, unable to move away from his roving tongue. She tossed her head to the right and left to try and get away from him, but it was hopeless.

Once again, he raised his arm, ready to hit her. She hoped he hit her hard, knocking her out so that she could sink into a black oblivion and never know what he did to her next. She looked him in the eye, willing him to do it. To hit her.

A sinister smile stretched his lips, his yellow teeth the last thing she saw as his hand connected with the side of her head and blackness engulfed her once again.

CHAPTER 12

Antonia's scream rent the air and Robot leaped to his feet from his crouched position ready to storm the shitty house where the asshole had taken her. A quick yank had him sitting on his ass in the dirt. He fired a *fuck off* look in Italy's direction.

The look bounced off his friend. They'd been in too many situations together to get offended by certain looks.

"I know you want to get in there, but I'm in charge of this mission. Sit your fucking ass down until the other guys are in place. We will get Antonia out, I *promise* you."

Robot blew out a frustrated breath and mentally counted to ten. Italy was right. This was a mission, they had a plan and they would stick to it. If he went in there, without thought or care, Antonia could get killed.

Fuck, he didn't want to think of her being killed, but that's what could be happening to her right now.

He and Italy had taken position in front of the house and had been squatting in the dirt for about fifteen minutes. While enroute to this place, Tex had contacted a SWAT team, and until they arrived, they had to sit tight. But if they didn't get here soon, he was going to tell Italy they were going in.

"Back is all clear. Noticed a room with a boarded up window. Best guess is that's where they've got Antonia. We're going to take the left side of the house." Cowboy spoke over the comms. He was teamed, like always, with Red.

"Sit-Rep, Joker?" Italy asked.

"Right side clear."

"How many perps are we looking at?"

"Four in the house including Antonia. T-Rex and I are waiting for your word."

Robot nudged Italy's foot. "How much longer till SWAT gets here?"

"Not long."

"I don't think I can wait much longer. Something's happened, I can feel it. It's too damn quiet now."

Italy adjusted his rifle and nodded. "Agree. If they're not here in sixty seconds we're going in."

Four *affirmatives* sounded in Robot's ear and he relaxed a fraction. He had no doubt he could count on his team. They'd been in many situations where time was of the essence. The difference between life and death could be a matter of seconds and every second they waited for the SWAT to arrive was a second Antonia didn't have.

Italy tapped him on the shoulder and he met his friend's eyes. A silent communication passed between them. Both men rose, and Italy murmured go, the signal for the rest of the team to get into position.

They crept toward the front. The front door wasn't closed properly. What the fuck were they thinking? Looking for a quick escape? Well, it worked to his advantage.

Once all the men were grouped together, Italy swung the door open and threw in two smoke cannisters in quick succession.

Footsteps thumped down the hallway. They took up position with their back to the wall. Through the haze of grey smoke two figures materialized. Joker and T-Rex knocked both men out with the butt of their rifles.

"Go. We've got these fuckers." Joker looked up as he grabbed some zip ties out of his pocket.

There were only two other people left, one was the woman he loved, and the other was the asshole who'd taken her. Robot would like nothing better than to put a bullet between his eyes so he couldn't hurt anyone else. The cops wouldn't like if he did that, they wanted the guy alive so they could question him, but while he breathed he was still a threat to Antonia.

"Take it easy, Robot. We'll do this the right way." Italy's words were words he'd said numerous times to other anxious members of the team. His instincts were right, Italy had the makings of a good team lead.

Together they crept down the hallway. Why hadn't the other guy come out to see what the fuss was all about?

"We're in here gentleman, come join the fun."

Robot's blood turned cold at the sound of the calm voice.

"Wait." Joker advised. "We'll be with you in two

seconds. These guys aren't going anywhere and SWAT just pulled up.

"Red," Robot spoke before giving Italy a chance. "Go out and advise them to wait for our signal before coming in. I don't trust this guy not to shoot Antonia."

"Affirmative."

"What are we going to do now?" asked Cowboy.

"Proceed as planned. As a group. There are five us to one of him. We'll take the fucker down and rescue Antonia." The resolve was clear in Italy's voice. Robot believed the same resolve thrummed through everyone on the team.

He took up his normal position at the front of the group, he wanted to be the first one Antonia saw. He lifted his hand and motioned forward.

They hugged the wall as they crept to the room at the back of the house. Reaching the doorway, he held up his fist.

"Gentleman, please there's no need for all this drama, come on in."

Robot entered the room, his eyes going straight to the bed and had to steel his spine at the scene in front of him. Antonia's face was puffy and blood streaked down either side from cuts on her forehead. He could see one knife protruding from her leg and another from her arm.

The man standing by the bed pointed a gun at her chest and the smile on his face suggested he was enjoying every single second.

This fucker was going to die.

In a split second Robot had his rifle at his eye and his finger squeezed the trigger. The man fell backwards as

Robot's bullet pierced him between the eye. He was also aware of another gun firing and bright red seeped into the front of his shirt.

Robot had no idea who fired the shot and he didn't care.

"Get the paramedics in here now," he shouted as he rushed over to Antonia's side. As much as he wanted to haul her in his arms, he controlled himself. He laid his head over her face, waiting for a warm puff of air to hit his cheek signifying that Antonia was still alive. Relief swamped him when he felt it.

Placing a hand over her heart he leaned close to her ear. "I'm here, T. I've got you. You're safe now."

In the background, he was aware of Italy dragging the body of the guy off Antonia and the sound of footsteps running down the hallway. He ignored it all.

"Sir, I need you to move so we can attend to the patient." A stranger's voice sounded over his shoulder. He ignored it.

"Sir, please we need to get to the patient." The voice insisted but now that he had Antonia back, he wasn't going to let anyone near her.

"Robot. Let the paramedics do their job. You're not helping Antonia." It was Cowboy's voice that finally got through the fog of despair he'd fallen into.

"Right, yes." He stood and moved to allow the men in to do their job.

Minutes passed, and he observed everything as if he was watching a movie. When the paramedics had transferred Antonia to a gurney, the knives still imbedded in her body he came back into his body and strode beside them as they wheeled her out.

He went to climb into the ambulance the paramedic who'd first spoke stopped him. "I'm sorry, sir, you can't ride with us."

Robot glared at the young paramedic, and he took a step back. "That's my wife. I'm *not* leaving her side." He brushed past the man and climbed into the back. He maneuvered himself so that he could sit by her head.

Once again, he took her hand, kissing it carefully so as not to disturb the IV needle on the top of her palm. He kissed her cheek. "Fight, T. I need you. I love you. Fight to come back to me."

ANTONIA DIDN'T WANT TO WAKE UP. BOSS WOULD ONLY hurt her more. As it was, every single part of her throbbed and her face felt as if it was ten times it's normal size. Had he used her as a punching bag while she'd been unconscious? The guy was a killer so of course he wouldn't have any issues taking advantage of a passed out woman.

Slowly the fuzz that coated her mind cleared, and she became aware of a constant beeping sound and there wasn't a spring digging in her back.

Her left hand was warmer than her right. Why was that? Nothing about her current situation seemed right.

Had Boss moved her?

She tried to open her eyes, but they seemed glued shut. Perhaps it was better she didn't open them, then she didn't have to see what hellhole she'd landed in.

Warm breath caressed her cheek and a familiar scent

wafted past her nose. Now she was imagining Robot was with her. She must be hallucinating.

"Are you awake, T?" The words whispered softly and reverently in her ear.

No, it couldn't be. Or could it?

Had her wish come true?

Had Robot found her?

"Robot?" Her mind formed the word, but she didn't think the message got to her mouth. She licked her dry lips and tried again. "Robot?"

Fingers caressed her forehead. "Yeah, T. I'm here. How are you feeling?"

How did she feel? That was a very good question. She didn't know how she felt. "I don't know. Everything hurts and I'm too scared to move."

The bed depressed beside her and a warm body aligned with hers. Memories of the last time she was in hospital assailed her memories. He'd done the exact same thing then as he was doing now. Unlike then, she welcomed his presence. Last time she'd shoved him and told him to get off her bed. Later she'd found out he stayed by her side until she'd woken up. Looks like he'd done the same thing again.

The need to see her husband, the man she loved, gave her the strength to will her eyes to open. She couldn't open them fully and her vision was blurry, but she could see her man. A soft smile played on his lips, but he looked awful.

His face was covered with blond scruff. He had dark rings under his eyes and the lines around his mouth and across his forehead were deeper than she'd ever seen them.

Love for the man lying next to her filled her until she was sure it was flowing out of her. "You look like shit."

That wasn't what she'd planned to say, but he chuckled. "There she is. There's my T."

He lips brushed hers and when he moved away, she moaned. "More."

"I would love to kiss you, but your lips are swollen and I don't want to hurt you anymore than you already are."

"Trust me when I say I'll take that pain." And she would. To have Robot's lips on her, when she feared she'd never feel them again, was worth any pain.

"Boss." She said his name on a gasp and Robot went from relaxed to combat ready beside her.

"Dead. I killed him."

Her mind was beginning to register that she was safe. "What happened?"

"It doesn't matter. It's over and he'll never hurt you or anyone else again."

Antonia understood why Robot was doing what he was. He was trying to protect her, but she needed to know what happened to her.

"Please Robot, tell me what happened. He stabbed me in the leg." A shudder rushed through her body as she recalled the pain of the knife entering her flesh. "The pain was so intense. So unbelievably intense and when he raised his arm to hit me again, I'd wished he would hit me hard enough to knock me out and he did. Tell me what he did to me after I was unconscious." She couldn't voice her biggest fear though. The words stuck in her throat.

"This is going to hurt," Robot warned before he lifted

her. Pain coursed through every part of her and she moaned loud, but the second Robot rested her against his hard chest and wrapped his arms tightly around her, every shard of glass breaking in her body was worth it. His warmth surrounded her and the sense of safety that only he could give her settled in her bones.

"Are you going to tell me now?"

She felt his sigh and waited. She'd rather hear whatever horrid things Boss did to her from him than from anyone else.

"I never want to remember what I walked in on ever again, but I know you need to know, so here goes." He smoothed his hand up and down her arm as far as he could without disturbing the various tubes and chords surrounding her. "Apart from the stab wound to your leg, he also stabbed your upper left arm. Slashed your legs and hit you a bit more around the face."

"That explains why I can't open my eyes." She swallowed and found the courage to ask the question she was afraid to know the answer to. "Did he—did he…"

Robot's finger placed a finger on her lips halting her stuttering attempt to speak. "No, T," he started softly. "He didn't do what you're thinking."

Tears leaked out of her swollen eyes. "Thank God."

Robot held her as she cried. A cleansing cry that washed away the horrid experience. Not completely, but for the moment the tears soothed her.

"I thought I'd lost you, T. It was bad enough when Bryan took you. But this time, this time I couldn't keep my emotions in check." With careful movements he laid her back down, the stabs of pain minimal this time. Robot turned on his side and faced her. Her breath hitched at the look in his eyes. "I walked into that room, saw what he did to you and didn't think, just acted. I lifted my gun and shot him between the eyes. I didn't care that the police wanted him alive. All I saw was a messed up fucker who hurt the woman I love, and I couldn't let him live."

Her mind took in everything he said, but her heart clamped down hard on four words and wouldn't let me go: *the woman I love.*

He loved her.

She lifted her hand and placed it on his cheek. "I knew in my heart you'd come for me. I knew all I had to do was hang on and you'd save me. Thank you for killing him. Thank you for saving me and thank you for loving me, because I love you, too, Brendan. So much."

Robot's blue eyes lit up at her declaration. His hand framed her face and a smile she'd never seen stretched his lips wide. "So, you wanna stay married to me? You're Vegas mistake?"

She laughed then winced, her ribs screaming at the motion. "Yes, I wanna stay married to you, my best Vegas bet."

Robot rested his forehead against hers. She loved these little touches. "I love you, T."

"Love you too, Brendan."

EPILOGUE

ANTONIA SAT at the table and sipped her champagne. Today had been a wonderful day. Carlos and Erin had gotten married in front of family and friends. The ceremony had been beautiful and there wasn't a dry eye in the church when they spoke their vows.

Fingers feathered down her arm and gooseflesh bubbled over her skin. She looked up and smiled at her husband. "Hey stranger." His lips brushed hers, and when he pulled away, she pouted. "That kiss was way too short, Mr. Dean."

Being best man and matron of honor, she and Robot had been busy looking after the bride and groom, and their time together during the day had been brief. Now that the end of the evening was upon them, they could relax with their duties and enjoy spending time together.

"If I did what I wanted to do to you, we'd be kicked out." He leaned over and kissed her neck.

Heat rushed to her core. She'd finally reached the stage of her recovery where her ribs didn't hurt if she breathed too hard. While they hadn't exactly been celibate during her convalescence, the type of sex they'd indulged in before her kidnapping hadn't been in the cards.

Tonight, though, she planned to thoroughly seduce her husband. "I'm going to hold you to that," she teased.

The music changed from the fast tempo to a slow love song. "Shall we dance, my love?" He stood and held out his hand.

"I'd love too."

They made their way to the dance floor. She spied Erin and Carlos wrapped up in each other's arms. Suzie and Joker were the same, their wedding was in a couple of weeks. Brielle and T-Rex were seated watching everyone, Antonia wondered why they weren't dancing but noticed the way T-Rex's hand rested protectively over her stomach.

"Is Brielle pregnant?"

Robot looked over at the couple. "I didn't think so, but by looking at their body language you might be right. T-Rex did say she'd quit her job. I wonder if this is why. I'll have to ask him at PT in a couple of days."

"No, don't pester him. They'll tell when they're ready. They may be waiting until they pass the twelve week mark."

Because of the wedding, the team was having a couple of days off from their normal routine. Antonia had plans to keep her man naked for those two days.

She snuggled into Robot's arms and they swayed

gently to the music. Her body grew warmer with every passing second and she tried to remember if there was a place she and Robot could sneak off to.

"Did you speak to the girl Cowboy brought to the wedding?"

Antonia looked over her shoulder and noticed the man in question dancing with his date. "Who Faith? Yeah, I met her briefly. From what I understand she's visiting Texas to check out a rodeo or it could be a rodeo horse she wants to buy. She mentioned she and Cowboy were on the circuit together when they were younger, before he joined the Navy."

"Really?" Robot cocked his head as he studied the couple. "Well, now that's interesting."

Antonia rolled her eyes. "I swear you guys all act like you're in high school. I bet you're going to give him a hard time about her when you see him next."

He winked at her. "You know me so well."

The music changed again and after a few seconds a chant started around the room.

"Robot."

"Robot."

"Robot."

Her husband groaned and shook his head.

"What?" she asked confused at his reaction. "What's going? Why are they chanting your name?"

"They want me to do the robot."

It took a second for Antonia to register what he was saying. A vague memory of him telling her something in Vegas entered her mind, but she wasn't sure. "Is that how you got your nickname?"

"Yes." He sighed heavily.

She burst out laughing. "Oh yes, please, *Robot*. I need to see if you truly deserve your moniker." The chant got louder. "Go on, do it for me, your loving wife."

He laughed, and pulled her tight against him kissing her quickly, but enough to heighten the desire flaring to life in her. "Only for you, my love. Only for you."

Robot handed her his jacket and made his way over to his teammates. She moved closer and laughed when he crooked his arm and bent to the side, just like a robot. Yep, he was pretty convincing after he made a few more moves.

He caught her eye and winked. She mouthed *I love you* and he responded with *you too*.

A few months ago, she'd wished she could turn back time to redo her Vegas mistake, now she wouldn't change a single thing about her life.

If you enjoyed this book please consider leaving a review. All reviews are greatly appreciated.

JOIN my Newsletter and find out about sales, free books, contests and new releases before anyone else!
Click HERE

You can read where the "Guardian Seals" all started with Protecting Lily. Click HERE

If you enjoy Sports Romances, check out my "The Elite"

series, featuring Olympic athletes. Grab the first book, Fighting to Win HERE

To find out about new releases and sales follow me on Bookbub. Follow me

ABOUT THE AUTHOR

On her very first school report her teacher said 'Nicole likes to tell her own stories'. Many years later she eventually sat down and wrote her first book.

Nicole writes sexy contemporary romances, seducing you one kiss at a time as you turn the pages. She enjoys taking two characters and creating unique situations for them.

Learn more about Nicole Flockton at http://www.nicoleflockton.com.

authornicole@nicoleflockton.com

ALSO BY NICOLE FLOCKTON

Guardian Seals

Protecting Lily

Protecting Maria

Guarding Erin

Guarding Suzie

Guarding Brielle

Guarding Antonia

Man's Best Friend

Blind Date Bet

The Elite

Fighting to Win

Fighting to Dream

Fighting for Love

Fighting for Redemption

The Freemasons

The Victor

The Hunter

Sweet Texas Secrets

Sweet Texas Fire

Sweet Texas Series Boxed Set

Bound Series

Bound by Her Ring

Bound by His Desire

Bound by Their Love

Bound by The Billionaire's Desire - Boxed Set

Lovers Unmasked Series

Masquerade

Rescuing Dawn

Seducing Phoebe

Emerald Springs Legacy Series

Daniel's Decision

Emerald Springs Legacy Collection

Barefoot Bay

Swipe for Mr. Right

Wrong Time for Mr. Right

Standalone Titles

White Knight (Co-Written with Abigail Owen)

Novellas

Tangled Vines

Melt My Heart Anthology

Tango Love

A Vacation Affair

Medal Up: A Winter Games Duology

Christmas in Ghost Gum Valley

There are many more books in this fan fiction world than listed here, for an up-to-date list go to www.AcesPress.com

You can also visit our Amazon page at: http://www.amazon.com/author/operationalpha

•

ALL the below books are in Kindle Unlimited!

Special Forces: Operation Alpha World

Denise Agnew: Dangerous to Hold
Shauna Allen: Awakening Aubrey
Shauna Allen: Defending Danielle
Shauna Allen: Rescuing Rebekah
Shauna Allen: Saving Scarlett
Shauna Allen: Saving Grace
Brynne Asher: Blackburn
Linzi Baxter: Unlocking Dreams
Jennifer Becker: Hiding Catherine
Alice Bello: Shadowing Milly
Julia Bright: Saving Lorelei
Julia Bright: Rescuing Amy
Victoria Bright: Surviving Savage
Victoria Bright: Going Ghost
Victoria Bright: Jostling Joker
Cara Carnes: Protecting Mari
Kendra Mei Chailyn: Beast
Kendra Mei Chailyn: Barbie
Kendra Mei Chailyn : Pitbull
Melissa Kay Clarke: Rescuing Annabeth
Melissa Kay Clarke: Safeguarding Miley

Samantha A. Cole: Handling Haven
Samantha A. Cole: Cheating the Devil
Sue Coletta: Hacked
Melissa Combs: Gallant
KaLyn Cooper: Rescuing Melina
Liz Crowe: Marking Mariah
Jordan Dane: Redemption for Avery
Jordan Dane: Fiona's Salvation
Riley Edwards: Protecting Olivia
Riley Edwards: Redeeming Violet
Riley Edwards Recovering Ivy
Riley Edwards: Romancing Rayne
Nicole Flockton: Protecting Maria
Nicole Flockton: Guarding Erin
Nicole Flockton: Guarding Suzie
Nicole Flockton: Guarding Brielle
Michele Gwynn: Rescuing Emma
Casey Hagen: Shielding Nebraska
Casey Hagen: Shielding Harlow
Casey Hagen: Shielding Josie
Casey Hagen: Shielding Blair
Casey Hagen: Trusting Jake
Desiree Holt: Protecting Maddie
Kathy Ivan: Saving Sarah
Kathy Ivan: Saving Savannah
Kathy Ivan: Saving Stephanie
Jesse Jacobson: Protecting Honor
Jesse Jacobson: Fighting for Honor
Jesse Jacobson: Defending Honor
Jesse Jacobson: Summer Breeze
Silver James: Rescue Moon

Silver James: SEAL Moon
Silver James: Assassin's Moon
Silver James: Under the Assassin's Moon
Becca Jameson: Saving Sofia
Kate Kinsley: Protecting Ava
Heather Long: Securing Arizona
Heather Long: Guarding Gertrude
Heather Long: Protecting Pilar
Heather Long: Covering Coco
Gennita Low: No Protection
Kirsten Lynn: Joining Forces for Jesse
Margaret Madigan: Bang for the Buck
Margaret Madigan: Buck the System
Margaret Madigan: Jungle Buck
Margaret Madigan: December Chill
Rachel McNeely: The SEAL's Surprise Baby
Rachel McNeely: The SEAL's Surprise Bride
Rachel McNeely: The SEAL's Surprise Twin
Rachel McNeely: The SEAL's Surprise Mission
KD Michaels: Saving Laura
KD Michaels: Protecting Shane
KD Michaels: Avenging Angels
Wren Michaels: The Fox & The Hound
Wren Michaels: The Fox & The Hound 2
Wren Michaels: Shadow of Doubt
Wren Michaels: Shift of Fate
Wren Michaels: Steeling His Heart
Kat Mizera: Protecting Bobbi
Mary B Moore: Force Protection
LeTeisha Newton: Protecting Butterfly
LeTeisha Newton: Protecting Goddess

LeTeisha Newton: Protecting Vixen
LeTeisha Newton: Protecting Heartbeat
MJ Nightingale: Protecting Beauty
MJ Nightingale: Betting on Benny
MJ Nightingale: Protecting Secrets
Sarah O'Rourke: Saving Liberty
Victoria Paige: Reclaiming Izabel
Anne L. Parks: Mason
Debra Parmley: Protecting Pippa
Debra Parmley: Split Screen Scream
Lainey Reese: Protecting New York
Rose Smith: Saving Satin
Jenika Snow: Protecting Lily
Harley Stone: Rescuing Mercy
Jen Talty: Burning Desire
Jen Talty: Burning Kiss
Jen Talty: Burning Skies
Jen Talty: Burning Lies
Jen Talty: Burning Heart
Megan Vernon: Protecting Us
Megan Vernon: Protecting Earth

Fire and Police: Operation Alpha World

Freya Barker: Burning for Autumn
KaLyn Cooper: Justice for Gwen
Aspen Drake: Sheltering Emma
Barb Han: Kace
Reina Torres: Justice for Sloane
Stacey Wilk: Stage Fright

As you know, this book included at least one character from Susan Stoker's books. To check out more, see below.

<u>Delta Force Heroes Series</u>

Rescuing Rayne (FREE!)

Rescuing Aimee (novella)

Rescuing Emily

Rescuing Harley

Marrying Emily

Rescuing Kassie

Rescuing Bryn

Rescuing Casey

Rescuing Sadie

Rescuing Wendy

Rescuing Mary

Rescuing Macie (April 2019)

<u>Badge of Honor: Texas Heroes Series</u>

Justice for Mackenzie (FREE!)

Justice for Mickie

Justice for Corrie

Justice for Laine (novella)

Shelter for Elizabeth

Justice for Boone

Shelter for Adeline

Shelter for Sophie

Justice for Erin

Justice for Milena

Shelter for Blythe

Justice for Hope

Shelter for Quinn (Feb 2019)
Shelter for Koren (June 2019)
Shelter for Penelope (Oct 2019)

SEAL of Protection Series

Protecting Caroline (FREE!)
Protecting Alabama
Protecting Fiona
Marrying Caroline (novella)
Protecting Summer
Protecting Cheyenne
Protecting Jessyka
Protecting Julie (novella)
Protecting Melody
Protecting the Future
Protecting Kiera (novella)
Protecting Dakota

SEAL of Protection: Legacy Series

Securing Caite
Securing Sidney (May 2019)
Securing Piper (Sept 2019)
Securing Zoey (TBA)
Securing Avery (TBA)
Securing Kalee (TBA)

New York Times, *USA Today* and *Wall Street Journal* Bestselling Author Susan Stoker has a heart as big as the state of Tennessee where she lives, but this all American girl has also spent the last fourteen years living in Missouri, California, Colorado, Indiana, and Texas. She's married to a retired Army man who now gets to follow *her* around the country.

She debuted her first series in 2014 and quickly followed that up with the SEAL of Protection Series, which solidified her love of writing and creating stories readers can get lost in.

If you enjoyed this book, or any book, please consider leaving a review. It's appreciated by authors more than you'll know.

www.stokeraces.com
www.AcesPress.com
susan@stokeraces.com

Made in United States
Cleveland, OH
20 November 2025

26328750R00105